Dominiqu... **ended long before the explosive touch of his lips on hers obliterated every coherent thought in her head.**

This was the full-blown, hungry kiss of a man caught in the grip of inflamed desire, and Dominique had never in her life been the recipient of such raw, passionate need. His tongue thrust into her mouth with almost brutal command, and a heat started to burn inside her that made her shake and fear for her very sanity.

Her hands reached out to steady herself against him, her fingers biting into the iron-hard flesh of his waist as her own escalating need suddenly outran any whispered caution in her head. She started to kiss Cristiano back just as feverishly and wantonly as he was kissing her, her heart open wide and her senses more intensely alive than they'd ever been before.

'I will lock the door,' Cristiano whispered.

Before she could absorb the earth-shattering meaning of such a statement he left her to do just that. Dominique stared at him as he returned, wondering how a man as beautiful and perfect as he could possibly want an unconfident and ordinary girl like her, when he could probably have any stunning woman he wanted…

The day **Maggie Cox** saw the film version of *Wuthering Heights*, with a beautiful Merle Oberon and a very handsome Laurence Olivier, was the day she became hooked on romance. From that day onwards she spent a lot of time dreaming up her own romances, secretly hoping that one day she might become published and get paid for doing what she loved most! Now that her dream is being realised, she wakes up every morning and counts her blessings. She is married to a gorgeous man, and is the mother of two wonderful sons. Her two other great passions in life—besides her family and reading/writing—are music and films.

Recent titles by this author:

THE RICH MAN'S LOVE CHILD
SECRETARY MISTRESS, CONVENIENT WIFE

THE SPANISH
BILLIONAIRE'S
CHRISTMAS
BRIDE

BY
MAGGIE COX

MILLS & BOON®
Pure reading pleasure™

First published in Great Britain 2008
Harlequin Mills & Boon Limited,
Eton House, 18-24 Paradise Road, Richmond, Surrey TW9 1SR

ISBN: 978 0 263 86485 4

Set in Times Roman 10½ on 13¼ pt
01-1208-39080

Printed and bound in Spain
by Litografia Rosés, S.A., Barcelona

THE SPANISH BILLIONAIRE'S CHRISTMAS BRIDE

To Suzy,
for your boundless enthusiasm and encouragement

CHAPTER ONE

DOMINIQUE couldn't believe what she was hearing. It was as if her worst nightmare had come to life. Still in shock from the news her mother had called to deliver, she was having trouble taking in the rest of the tirade.

'Let me get this straight,' she said to her mother. 'You told Cristiano Cordova where I lived so that he could come and see the baby and… What was it you said? See for himself the dreadful conditions in which I'm living?'

She stared at the telephone receiver in her hand as though it were an unexploded bomb, mute outrage gripping her throat while fear and dread cascaded through her bloodstream like a swollen river bursting its banks.

'Why? Why would you do such a thing?'

'Why do you think? I told him because the Cordovas obviously aren't short of a penny or two, and they *owe* you! Since that good-for-nothing Ramón is dead, and you've been saddled with his child to try and raise on your own instead of finishing your degree, they ought to take some sort of responsibility for what's happened, wouldn't you say?'

'Is that what you told him? That he was responsible for Matilde?'

'Yes!' There was stubborn defiance in the other woman's voice. 'And he agreed!'

'Listen…they owe me nothing! It was my own decision to go ahead with the pregnancy and have the baby, and it's nothing to do with anyone else! If Ramón himself wasn't interested in his daughter why do you think for one moment that I would be remotely interested in making contact with the rest of his family? Much less have one of them come visit me!'

'Well, someone should pay for the mess that man got you into—and why shouldn't his family cough up? He ruined your life, Dominique! You were on course for a wonderful career and now look at you!'

For a moment Dominique couldn't speak over the raw pain inside her throat. Her mother made it sound as if she was the biggest failure that ever lived! Was there nothing she could ever do to please her? Already knowing the answer, she fought off the wave of shame and despondency that washed over her and dispiritedly murmured a strained goodbye.

* * *

A week on and still she greeted each minute in dread of Cristiano Cordova showing up at her door, possibly wanting to assume some sort of control over her baby's future. The already broken nights she endured, waking to feed Matilde, had been disrupted further by anxiety and fear. The freedom to lead her own life that she'd so desperately sought when she'd finally left her mother's house to care for her baby on her own had been horribly threatened and spoiled.

She had already been feeling strangely disconnected from the rest of the world—the only light in her life being derived from her beautiful baby girl—while other people were looking forward to the holiday season, busy flitting in and out of the shops that were bursting with glittering arrays of Christmas paraphernalia, and counting down the days for the big event itself. The restaurant where Dominique worked as a waitress was already inundated with orders for lunch on Christmas Day, and she could have increased her hours in a heartbeat if she didn't fiercely guard the maximum time she could afford to spend with her baby. But other people's anticipation of Christmas only served to heighten her sense of isolation.

And now her mother had betrayed her. She had colluded with Cristiano Cordova—Ramón's rich and influential cousin—behind her back, and encouraged the idea that Dominique's baby was now *his* responsibility, since there was now no hope of Ramón himself ever fulfilling that role. The revelation still had the power to stun her senseless. She was still reeling from the news that Ramón was dead…killed in a car accident on some remote mountain pass in Spain. The catalogue of heartbreak since Dominique had met him was surely now complete?

Cristiano declined the offer of more coffee from the smiling air stewardess and, making a steeple of his fingers, stared out at the dazzling vista of pale clouds that resembled sun-struck snow-covered mountain peaks in the sky. For a poignant moment he imagined his young cousin's restless and unhappy spirit, roaming free amongst those self-same clouds—no longer bound by the constraints of the physical existence that had seemed to cause him so much turmoil and difficulty while he lived… Emotion welled up inside him and painfully cramped his throat. *If only he had been able to get through to Ramón as he'd longed to…get him to see that the family would have forgiven him every transgression if he had only met them halfway…*

But it was too late for recriminations. The situation was *beyond* rescue now. Cristiano had never voiced out loud his terrible fear that perhaps Ramón had *deliberately* sought to end his own life by driving his car over a clifftop that dreadful night—but he could not help thinking it just the same, and the thought gave him nightmares.

When a letter had been discovered amongst Ramón's things after the funeral—from a girl none of the family had ever even *heard* of before—Cristiano and the family had honestly been stunned by its contents. The girl…*Dominique*…wrote to tell him news of the birth of her baby—*Ramón's* baby—and had even included a photograph of the infant. Although things were well and truly over between them, she wrote, she thought he should at least know that he was the father of a healthy and beautiful little girl.

The letter had been dated six months earlier, and though he knew he would have to go to the UK and investigate for himself the legitimacy of the girl's claims, Cristiano had also realised it must fall to him to convey the news that Ramón was dead—and that could not wait. But he had not had the opportunity to speak to Dominique herself. Instead, when he had called the telephone number she'd included in her letter, the girl's mother had answered. Upon his revealing to her who he was and why he was calling the woman had not held back.

His 'heartless, good-for-nothing cousin' had wrecked her daughter's life, Cristiano had been told in no uncertain terms, and his family had better do something about it. Dominique had only had a year to go before she finished her degree, and had had a bright future to look forward to. Now, instead, she was weighed down with the responsibilities of a baby!

When Jean Sanderson had calmed down sufficiently for him to get a word in edgeways Cristiano had soothingly but authoritatively told her that if it were true that her daughter's baby was Ramón's then he would of course take steps to ensure their future prospects were comfortable and to her liking. Certainly Dominique would not be denied the opportunity to finish her education. The Cordova family took their responsibilities seriously and would not turn their backs on one of their own. Slightly placated, Mrs Sanderson had then volunteered Dominique's new address—she had apparently moved out since her letter to Ramón—and was living in a 'grubby little bedsit' in one of London's least attractive boroughs.

The accusations had come hard and fast. Dominique's mother's anger and resentment were glaringly evident. *Even in death it seemed that Ramón's reckless and thoughtless behaviour was still having massive repercussions on people's lives...*

Yet again it had been left to Cristiano to smooth the troubled waters his cousin had left in his wake.

Releasing a troubled sigh, he pulled his gaze

away from the spectacular view offered by the small window beside him and concerned himself instead with thoughts of his family. A family whose sorrow at losing a beloved son had been unexpectedly eased by the revelation that he'd fathered a child…a child they hoped and prayed Cristiano would be bringing back with him on his return—*back where they were convinced she belonged…*

There was a knock at the door, and in the same instant the milk she'd been heating on the stove for hot chocolate boiled over. Cursing softly, Dominique turned off the gas, surveyed the burnt sticky mess clinging to the side of the saucepan, and unhappily mourned the diminishing ability of her once sharp brain to concentrate for even two seconds flat. The trouble was Matilde was teething, and they had both had a horrendously sleepless night. Now fed, and finally asleep, the baby lay cosily wrapped up against the cold in her cot, and Dominique had been looking forward to the comfort of a hot drink for herself.

No doubt the person knocking on the door at that inopportune moment was Katie—the ballet student who lived in the bedsit opposite. Frequently out of milk, sugar, tea, coffee…*food*—anything you cared to name—she often walked across the landing to see if Dominique could help out. Leaving the cramped space that laughingly masqueraded as a kitchen and padding across the thin, worn carpet in her stockinged feet, Dominique opened the door with a resigned smile already in place—and a swift, silent prayer of thanks that she had done her shopping yesterday, before Matilde's teething problem had kept them both awake for half the night...

'Dominique Sanderson?'

She stared up at the imposing male on the other side of the door with her heart racing a mile a minute. He was obviously foreign—even if his accent hadn't alerted her to the fact, his dark and striking looks strongly confirmed it—and Dominique half closed the door again, feeling sick with dread. 'Who wants to know?' she answered, the smile she had automatically summoned for Katie firmly banished.

'I am Cristiano Cordova...Ramón Cordova's cousin. May I come in and speak with you?' he enquired formally.

'No, you can't!' In a panic, Dominique glanced over at the tattered Chinese screen behind which her infant daughter's cot was positioned—grateful that at this angle it was completely hidden from view. 'It was very wrong of my mother to give you my address, and I told her so! I'm sorry, but you're just going to have to turn around and go back to wherever you came from. Because although you want to speak to me, I do *not* want to speak to you!'

She went to shut the door, but he was too quick for her and grabbed the edge with a grip like steel. Dominique gasped.

'If you shut the door in my face I promise you I will wait outside all night if I have to!' the man warned. 'And I do not make idle promises. So, if you want to avoid the embarrassment of explaining the reason for my presence to your neighbours, I suggest you simply let me come in and talk quietly to you in private.'

Seeing by his steely-eyed, hard-jawed expression that he was more than capable of carrying out an all-night vigil if she went back inside and closed the door, Dominique reluctantly moved away to allow him entrance. Her legs had gone to jelly, and she wondered how she even managed that small feat.

As the tall Spaniard came in through the door she couldn't help glaring at him. From the moment her mother had announced she'd given him her address—and implied that he and his family were now responsible for her predicament—Dominique had been quite prepared to dislike him and all he stood for intensely. After all, hadn't she already had a bitter example of how his family could behave in Ramón? Why should this man be any less heartless?

Even though her first view of him was through a red mist of anger, she saw nothing in the striking bronzed face with its sleek, taut lines to change her mind in any way. All she saw was another unwanted authority figure who believed it was his God-given right to try and take control of her and her baby's life, and she wanted to physically push him out the door and yell at him never to come back.

'What do you want to talk to me about?' she demanded, folding her arms to try and still the tremors that had seized her.

'The baby, of course…and the fact that her father was my cousin, who is now dead. There are things to discuss relating to both these matters.'

'Well, I don't want you here. Can't you see that? Ramón and I broke up several months ago, and he couldn't have cared less when I told him I was pregnant! I'm really sorry if you've had a wasted journey, but I didn't ask you to come in the first place!'

'No…you did not ask me to come,' Cristiano Cordova replied, his voice smooth but with a rich undertone that made Dominique's senses snap to attention. 'But I would very much be failing in my duty to Ramón if I had elected to stay in Spain and ignore his baby's existence. I found your letter, and I am aware of all that has happened. Now I am here to help alleviate some of the considerable stress and worry you must undoubtedly be under in such a difficult situation.'

'You're not going to take Matilde away from me, so don't even *think* it!'

Stepping boldly in front of the six feet plus frame that exuded a bearing nothing less than regal—even here, in her deplorably shabby little bedsit with its threadbare floor covering and faded ancient wallpaper—Dominique was enraged at even the mere thought of such a possibility. She might only be twenty-one, but she still had rights—even if nobody else seemed to think so!

'I think you need to calm yourself, Dominique. How can we discuss anything if you are in such a state of agitation? Perhaps we should start over again?' The Spaniard considered her gravely for a moment, before extending his hand and letting his previously solemn mouth curve briefly into a smile. 'It is unfortunate that our paths should only cross after such a tragic turn of events, but even so…I am very pleased to meet you, Dominique.'

Dominique warned herself not to be won over by the appearance of warmth and charm. Ramón had once told her that his rich and powerful cousin could be described as 'dynamite in a silk glove', and that people would do well not to be deceived by his amenable exterior and underestimate him. She remembered Ramón had sounded impressed when he'd revealed this—as though he *envied* his cousin's gravitas and power. Apparently he was a man with a formidable reputation—and not just professionally. Cristiano commanded great respect and admiration from all those who knew him, and in the hallowed circle of the influential and respected his word and opinion was *law*.

A tiny shiver scudded down her spine as his large hand with its sprinkling of fine dark hair across the knuckles enfolded hers. His eyes were black as impenetrable caves, fringed with luxuriant sable lashes, and for a suspended moment Dominique was magnetised by them.

'Well…' She pulled her hand free as quickly as possible, to dispel the sense of deep disquiet that rippled through her, and took a step back. 'All I want is to be left alone to raise my child in peace. Ramón's family are under no obligation to help me in any way. It was my decision to have her, and I'm certainly not looking for hand-outs from his relatives!'

Her imposing visitor held up his hand as if to restore calm, the gesture conveying all the authority and command of Moses overseeing the parting of the Red Sea. His dark gaze was pensive as he focused it on Dominique. 'Your bid for independence is admirable… but I have to tell you that there are certain things about our family that you *must* understand, and one of them is that we have a code of honour that must be upheld in all circumstances. Part of that code is that we take care of our own.'

Clearly Ramón had missed that memo, Dominique thought wryly. As much as she had judged Ramón for his lack of responsibility, now she could not help resenting his cousin's presence with a vengeance. But the formidably broad shoulders encased by the superbly tailored jacket he wore over a black cashmere sweater seemed to signify an indomitable fortress that she had no hope of breaching, and she suddenly knew without a shadow of a doubt that this proud, handsome Spaniard had no intention of going quietly away and leaving her to manage Matilde on her own.

Her heart slammed up against her ribcage in alarm. 'I told you—I don't want anyone's help! Least of all help from the family of a man who proved anything *but* honourable!'

She had sandy brown hair fashioned into one long silky plait that fell over a slender shoulder, eyes the colour and appearance of a placid blue lake on a summer's day, and features that might easily have been the inspiration for any of the Grand Masters if she had but been born in another century.

The realisation of how *young* she was hit Cristiano like an iron fist. Ramón himself had only been twenty-five, but even so...Dominique Sanderson barely looked out of the schoolroom! What had his thoughtless irresponsible cousin been thinking of when he took up with such an innocent and why hadn't he protected her from possible consequences when he had decided to seduce her?

He fielded the strong sense of outrage that unexpectedly burned inside him and mentally stored it for contemplation at a more appropriate time. Despite that, a muscle at the side of his temple continued to throb with tension. The girl presented a challenge. He knew now she was not going to be easily won over and persuaded to accept the aid that was due to her and, confessing silent surprise at that, Cristiano sensed he had a battle on his hands.

There were two well-worn tapestry-covered armchairs, one either side of a fireplace that housed an inadequate electric bar heater rather than a comforting glowing fire, and he gestured towards them. 'Let us sit down, shall we? Now, tell me…where did you get the astonishing idea that I came to try and take the child away from you?'

'Didn't you?'

'Of course not! A child belongs with her mother—unless that mother is unfit, of course—and that is where she should stay.'

'I am a *good* mother!' She sat forward in her chair suddenly, and Cristiano could tell by the way the muscles in her face were working that she was having trouble keeping back her emotions. 'We may not live in the lap of luxury, but I work hard and do my best, and I would die rather than let my baby come to harm in any way!'

Cristiano frowned. 'Please…do not distress

yourself. Your ability as a mother is not in question. Regarding why I am here: I told your mother that as the head of the Cordova family I see it as my duty to oversee the care and protection of my cousin's child, since he has so sadly died, and I naturally extend that care and protection to include you too, Dominique.'

'I don't need anybody's care and protection! I can manage quite well on my own, thank you!'

Her huge blue eyes were suddenly bathed in tears, but Cristiano quickly realised that the reaction was born out of fury and frustration rather than self-pity.

'My mother only wants rid of the baby…can't you tell? She wants me to go back to university and complete my degree as if nothing has changed! She sees Matilde as an inconvenience that needs to be dealt with, and that's why she jumped at the chance to invite you over here! I think she was really hoping that you would take Matilde away!'

'I am very sorry to hear that. But if that is true, then it only confirms my opinion that you and your daughter would be better off returning with me to Spain than remaining here in England. If Ramón were still alive, I am certain he would come to that conclusion too, given time.' *He was not certain about that at all, but Cristiano would say anything he had to if it would help him achieve the outcome he desired.*

'I want you to know that I told him I would never make any claims on him regarding the baby. It was clear he didn't want her right from the start, so why would I humiliate myself by pursuing some sort of recompense? Besides…having Matilde was my decision and my decision alone. Becoming a father and being responsible for another human being—even his own child—held no appeal for Ramón whatsoever.'

'I do not doubt it!' Cristiano returned acidly. 'But it is a shame he did not think of that before he impregnated you!'

She blushed, and the sight of that subtle spread of pink fanning across her smooth pale cheeks, and the way her innocent unadorned mouth parted softly in surprise, caused an acute charge of electricity to explode in the pit of his stomach. It so disturbed him that for a moment Cristiano lost his train of thought.

'It wasn't all his fault. I was equally as foolish… as reckless—though I don't regret having my baby for a second!'

Frankly incredulous at her immediate defence of his wayward cousin—especially when he had to all intents and purposes abandoned her—Cristiano flattened his hands over his knees as he released an impatient irritated sigh. 'I am appalled that he did not make proper provision for you and his daughter whether he wanted to be in your lives or not! How did he expect you to support the baby when you were still a student and living at home with your mother?'

A tiny furrow appeared just above the bridge of her nose, and her slim hands moved restlessly in her lap. 'He probably didn't think about it much, if the truth were known. But I want you to know that I *am* supporting my baby quite adequately without him! Just before I left home I got myself a job. I waitress five nights a week at a local restaurant, and my friend Marie minds Matilde for me while I'm working.'

So that was how she earned her living and paid for this inhospitable room.

Instantly any fear Cristiano might have played in his mind that Dominique could turn out to be some opportunist gold-digger, seeking a chance to be financially supported for life once she knew Ramón's family was wealthy, was completely rendered null and void. She simply did not seem capable of such subterfuge. And someone looking to benefit from the Cordova estate would hardly try and slam the door in his face when he turned up on the doorstep, would they? She was *not* the kind of girl he'd been expecting to meet at all. She was the polar opposite of the other immature females Ramón had played fast and loose with in his short and disreputable life! Instead of sulky demands she radiated a quiet dignity and resolve that was impressive in one so young.

Cristiano felt the renewed throb of painful

tension pulsating in his temple like a relentless drumbeat as he glanced round once more at the poor state of the room he was in. It looked clean enough, but its aging furniture and fittings and inadequate heating made his stomach clench in dismay. Considering the child, he guessed she must be with this friend of Dominique's right now, because there was no sign of her. A shame. He had very much been looking forward to seeing her.

'Faced with the reality of how you live—' he frowned '—I would dispute your assertion that you are managing even adequately. These are clearly not the kind of circumstances conducive to raising a child and giving her the sense of security and comfort that she deserves! Especially when her father came from a privileged and wealthy background with a family who would have moved heaven and earth to help him if he had only come to us and revealed the truth of his impending fatherhood!'

'I got the feeling Ramón didn't like the idea of being under any sort of obligation to his family.'

'Under an obligation?' Cristiano hardly knew how he stayed sitting in his seat. His expression was formidably grim. *This* from a man whose proclivity for taking what he wanted—no matter who it hurt—had been second nature? A man who had been busy squandering his inheritance on fast living and reckless and sometimes dangerous pursuits without a care for anyone but himself right up until the day he died!

'Anyway…whatever people think of him…he's dead now, isn't he? He's not here to defend himself against what anybody says any more.' Her faultless blue eyes momentarily dazzled Cristiano with the flare of pain he saw reflected there.

'Yes, he is dead.' Feeling as though someone had taken a sledgehammer to his middle with this distressing reminder, he momentarily rubbed at the tension that had now extended to the front of his brow. 'Which is even more reason why this completely unacceptable situation cannot continue. Having met you, and acquainted myself with your situation, I have no doubt in my mind that you and the child must return with me to Spain,' he announced commandingly, rising to his feet.

CHAPTER TWO

'Now, wait a minute!' It was Dominique's turn to jump to her feet. 'Before you get too carried away, don't you think you ought to listen to what *I* want? This is my life we're talking about here…mine and my daughter's!'

'I am well aware of that, and I am only suggesting this solution because I have your best interests at heart! And because, as far as I am concerned, your child is a Cordova and should be where she belongs—enjoying the advantages of her birthright in Spain, with a family who will love and cherish her!'

'*I* love and cherish her!'

'And what about the rest of your family?'

'There's only my mother.'

'And clearly from what I have heard so far your mother does *not* love and cherish your daughter, and that is *not* an acceptable state of affairs!'

The beautiful face in front of Cristiano drained

of colour, but he felt no remorse for simply stating the truth. He saw his solution to this predicament as imperative, and had to admit that his family had been absolutely right when they had declared that Ramón's child belonged with them.

'But Spain…?'

'It is hardly a million miles away.' He allowed himself an ironic little smile. 'In these days when you can catch a plane to anywhere almost at the drop of a hat the world grows ever smaller, no?'

'It's just that—'

'You are concerned about not finishing your education, perhaps? Your mother indicated that was a big regret for you. Let me allay your worries on that score. I will be quite happy to pay for the rest of your education, Dominique, and there will be no shortage of offers to help take care of Matilde so that you can study, I assure you! We have some wonderful universities in Spain, and I see no reason why you cannot complete your degree there.'

'Well, my mother misled you, *Señor* Cordova. Not completing my degree was *her* big regret—not mine! I'm a mother now, and that's my first priority. And even if I did want to go back to university I certainly wouldn't be happy to have you foot the bill for it!'

Again Cristiano was struck by how fiercely independent and proud she was, and his unexpected feeling of admiration was genuinely disturbing. It was far from the way he had expected to be feeling at this meeting—in fact, he had prepared himself for the worst.

'In that case I cannot see that there are any obstacles whatsoever to prevent you from coming to reside in Spain.'

'Can't you? Well, you're not me, are you? And I have lots of doubts about the whole idea—despite what you say!'

'Listen to me!' Calmness suddenly gave way to the frustration and impatience Cristiano had hardly realised he was harbouring. 'You are not the only one to think about in this distressing situation! Ramón's mother is desperate to see the baby. She has lost her only son and is destroyed! Learning that he fathered a child has helped give her solace in the midst of her terrible grief. Would you deny her that solace, Dominique?'

She looked stricken. Then she made an agitated movement with her hand, before lifting it anxiously to her throat. 'I know so little about how he was killed…will you tell me more?'

Even though he'd known this was coming, Cristiano was still ill prepared to relive the disturbing events of that night, and his mouth flattened grimly. *He silently resolved to keep the explanation as brief as possible.*

'He was driving too fast on a hazardous

mountain road in the early hours of the morning,' he intoned, his tongue feeling thick in his mouth. 'The light was poor, and the investigation concluded that he probably lost control of the car on a sharp bend that no doubt took him by surprise. It would have happened very quickly and he was probably killed outright. His car was found at the bottom of a cliff the next morning by a couple walking on the beach. The coroner recorded a verdict of accidental death. I cannot tell you any more than that.'

Cannot or *will* not? Inside Dominique despair set in. Ramón might have died in considerable pain. She might have stopped loving him a long time ago, but he'd still been the father of her baby. She wrapped her arms around her chest to hold in her grief.

Needing to divert her unhappiness, she grasped at what Cristiano had said previously. 'I understand how much his mother must want to see Matilde, and I am truly sorry for her suffering…the poor woman must be demented at losing her only son! But Christmas is just a couple of weeks away, and it's the busiest time of year at the restaurant I work at. You must understand that I have responsibilities too, and if I were to go to Spain I couldn't possibly go until the New Year.'

His black eyes stared at her in disbelief. 'You would put this unimportant job you have in a restaurant before letting a grieving woman see her only grandchild?'

His lip curled contemptuously, and Dominique flinched at the scorn in his voice.

'Unimportant? It's the means of earning my living so that I can provide for Matilde and me! You might not be aware, but job opportunities aren't exactly overflowing for women in my situation, so don't you *dare* look at me as if I'm deliberately creating problems where there aren't any!'

'You talk about opportunity…can you not see that is exactly what I am offering you by suggesting you move to Spain? There we can provide opportunities that will improve your lives a hundredfold.'

Moving onto her opposite hip, Dominique scraped her hand wearily through her hair. 'Even if I agreed to go with you and meet Ramón's mother and his family you must understand it could only be for a short visit. You can hardly expect me to just leave everything behind and decamp to another country as though I was just moving round the corner! And to go and live with a bunch of strangers too!'

'They would not be strangers for very long. They are warm, loving people, and they would embrace you as though you were one of their own—which, of course, by virtue of being the mother of Ramón's child, you are. It is a shame your own mother could not be as forthcoming! I have heard myself her obvious antagonism towards you for taking a path she did not want by bearing the child of a man she clearly despised. The sooner you and the baby are far away from such a woman the better, as far as I am concerned!'

Cristiano's words hit their mark. The relationship between Dominique and her mother had deteriorated to an all-time low from the moment Dominique had confessed her pregnancy, and even Matilde's arrival had not softened the other woman's heart in any way. She refused to even *hold* the baby, let alone mind her for any length of time! Her lack of affection had blighted Dominique's own childhood, and it was heartbreaking that she was now treating her grandchild in the same cruel way. Yet even so…it would be a hell of a gamble to go and live with the family of a man Dominique knew had never loved her, who had callously turned his back on her when he'd found out she was pregnant.

'I'm sorry… But, like I said, I can't go *anywhere* until after the New Year—and then only for a visit.'

'So you say.'

'I've explained my reasons. Why won't you—?'

'Where is the baby tonight? With this friend of yours?' Cristiano interrupted. 'I was very much hoping to see her.'

The annoyance in his voice was clear, and Dominique felt her body tighten even more in response. 'She's not with my friend.'

'Then where is she?'

'She's right here…asleep in her cot behind that screen. It helps shut out the light a little, so it won't disturb her.'

She was already moving towards the other side of the room, and Cristiano followed her with a stunned look on his face. Dominique knew she could have deceived him by agreeing that the baby *was* with her friend, but whilst she was afraid to let him see Matilde for fear of future demands, in all conscience she knew she could not refuse his request. As overwhelming as the thought was, Cristiano Cordova was part of her daughter's family.

'Here she is. She's teething at the moment— that's why her cheeks look so pink.' She heard the love and pride in her own voice as she stood to the side to allow Cristiano a better view.

The sleeping infant looked blissfully peaceful and angelic as Cristiano peered into the cot to gaze at her. With her cap of sable hair, sweet little face and dimpled chin—a *definite* genetic inheritance from the Cordovas—she was absolutely enchanting. For disturbing seconds his head swam and his heart raced as he remembered another infant—had she lived, she would have been just like her. Then he recalled the fact that this was *Ramón's* baby, and that his cousin would never enjoy the privilege of gazing at his beautiful daughter as Cristiano was gazing at her now. Once again, sadness and regret bore down on him like a heavy iron cloak laid across his shoulders.

Glancing up, he solemnly studied the pale, strained features of the girl standing beside him. He could scarcely think of her as a woman at all—she appeared no more than a teenager.

'She is exquisite,' he remarked, the corners of his mouth lifting into a smile despite the terrible circumstances that had brought him here.

'She's a contented, happy soul. I can sense that about her already.'

Her guard down, Dominique ventured a smile back, and Cristiano thought he had never seen eyes of that vivid *heavenly* blue before. The mesmerising colour was tempting him to dive down deep into their iridescent crystal depths and lose himself completely. Young or not, there was something about her that affected him deeply, and the leap of hunger that suddenly flared inside him shockingly confirmed it.

'She must be—what? Around six…seven months old now?'

'Nearly seven, yes.'

'She is much changed from the picture you sent with your letter to Ramón.'

'I'd only just had her then. She was a tiny pink scrunched-up little thing, but she was still the most beautiful creature I'd ever seen!' Coiling her long honey-brown plait round her fingers, Dominique sighed and let it go again. 'It's such a shame that Ramón couldn't bring himself to acknowledge her. Not for my sake but for Matilde's. A child deserves to know her father, or at least something about him, don't you think?'

The statement had a doubly poignant resonance for her. Her own father had left her mother when Dominique was just a baby, and her mother had always refused to talk about him except to run him down. No matter how she personally felt about Ramón, Dominique would never do that to her own child.

Reaching inside the cot, she tenderly ran the tip of her finger across the sleeping baby's downy cheek. 'I think she'd make any man proud to be her father.' Her voice was an emotional whisper as her glistening eyes met Cristiano's.

'Yes…she would…'

Suddenly Cristiano realised he was weary right down to his marrow, and not as in charge of his emotions as he would like. Although no stranger to the deadening weight of grief, he had honestly forgotten how enervating it could be. Now tiredness and sorrow was draining him of the capacity to stay clear-headed and in control, and this girl with her flawless blue eyes and stubborn pride was disturbing things in him that he would prefer remained dormant.

His thoughts inevitably turned to his family. He knew that they were waiting anxiously to hear about the success of his trip so that they could make preparations for welcoming Dominique and the baby into their home. Despite Dominique's reservations about returning to Spain with him, Cristiano had no intention of disappointing them.

'It is getting late.' Glancing down at the gold Cartier watch that glinted expensively against his tanned wrist, he deliberately assumed a more businesslike manner to help put things back on an even keel. 'I need to book into my hotel and get a shower and some dinner. Tomorrow I will send a car for you, and we can meet to discuss the situation further when we are both feeling a little less emotional and overwrought. Do you agree?'

'I'll agree for Ramón's mother's sake,' Dominique replied, moving stiffly towards the door. 'But I'm not promising anything more than that.

Biting back his frustration, Cristiano reached inside his jacket pocket, withdrew his wallet, and then a small embossed card. 'This is the name and telephone number of where I am staying. If you should think of anything you need before we meet tomorrow…*anything* at all…I want you to ring me.

I will send the car at around ten a.m. Will that suit? The sooner we can talk again the better.'

'Ten is fine. I'm always up early with Matilde.'

'So…I will say goodbye for now, and look forward to seeing you again tomorrow, Dominique.'

He extended his hand to her and she took it reluctantly, slipping her palm away from contact with his as soon as she could, as if she was wary of his touch and his promises. Cristiano's shoulders stiffened. He nodded towards her rather curtly, to show his displeasure at this small act of rebellion, and ruefully made his exit.

Dominique asked for Cristiano at the desk and was stunned by the deferential response she received. No sooner did she mention his name than a smartly suited concierge arrived to whisk her personally up to the top floor in the spacious lift of the glamorous Mayfair hotel. He left her outside the door of his suite with all the respectful attention that any visiting VIP might receive.

Feeling somewhat overwhelmed, Dominique waited until her escort departed before she touched her knuckles to the walnut panelling and knocked. As she did so, she would have sworn that her heartbeat was far louder than the answering echo that seemed to bounce ominously round the wide, softly carpeted corridor. She had never set foot in such a smart, exclusive hotel before, and couldn't help but feel like an impostor. And the prospect of seeing Cristiano again after the turbulent encounter of last night was growing ever more daunting.

When the shiny black chauffeur-driven Jaguar had arrived to pick her up and bring her here it had sent Dominique's fears spiralling almost out of control. Now here, in these luxurious, opulent surroundings, her concerns about the power the Cordovas might potentially have over her were frighteningly confirmed. She'd hardly slept a wink for thinking about the Spaniard's visit. *Had Cristiano been telling her the truth when he'd said that Ramón's family would welcome her and Matilde with open arms?* What if it had just been a ruse to get her on Spanish soil where, with their money and power, they could bring the full force of the legal system to bear to ensure that Matilde stayed with them for ever?

'Dominique.'

Suddenly the man she'd come to visit was in the open doorway before her—a tall, dark clothed figure, lean-hipped and hard-muscled, the suggestion of reined-in power very much evident despite his casual stance. Like a cat ready to pounce at the first hint of danger. Glancing up into his compelling face, she saw that his eyes were as fathomless as a black night studded with stars, and his jet hair gleamed like a dark moonlit sea. Dominique's mouth seemed to instantly dry up at the sight of him.

'Where is Matilde?'

'I left her with my friend for a couple of hours…I thought it would make it easier for us to talk.'

'That is a shame. I was looking forward to seeing her again.'

Dominique felt both guilty and chastised. 'I'm not trying to stop you seeing her. I just thought—'

'It is early yet. Perhaps I can see her later on in the day?'

Cristiano studied her face intently for a moment, as though needing to discern whether he could trust her or not, and Dominique sensed he knew she had not brought Matilde along because her fears about the outcome of this meeting had not yet been allayed.

'You had better come in.'

The elegant drawing room she entered was decorated in a tasteful quintessentially English style, with antique furniture, inviting luxurious sofas and armchairs, and plush red velvet curtains finished with opulent swags at the windows. There was even a baby grand piano in residence, its polished ebony wood gleaming. Dominique felt like the little match girl, wandering in from the cold in her nondescript black woollen dress and slightly over-sized tweed coat. A room like this, she mused, called for nothing less than a tall elegant blonde clad in haute couture and diamonds—the kind that graced billboards, not a five-foot-five unconfident girl with nondescript brown hair and a deepening sense of dread.

'I've ordered us some coffee. It should be with us shortly. Please…let me take your coat.'

Embarrassed and then angry at the idea that Cristiano must guess that her well worn, less-than-elegant coat was a charity shop buy, Dominique handed it to him with an air of defiance.

'Sit down,' he told her, his dark gaze briefly skimming her figure in the unremarkable black dress…*another cast-off from a charity shop.*

It was impossible to know what was going on behind those extraordinary dark eyes of his, but everything about Cristiano Cordova reeked of class and money. Standing there in that elegant drawing room with him, Dominique was painfully aware of the discrepancy in their backgrounds. It was funny, but she hadn't felt that way with Ramón. Maybe it was because he had been younger and a little less sure of himself? There had been times in their short-lived relationship when he had definitely displayed what had seemed like vulnerability to her. In contrast, she had never met a man who appeared more certain of his place in the world than Cristiano

Cordova. No doubt he already *had* a tall elegant blonde in his life, Dominique mused.

'Make yourself comfortable,' he suggested. 'It is cold outside today, no?'

He didn't seem the type to casually discuss the weather, and she guessed that maybe he was doing it to try and help her feel less overwhelmed. But would a man like him be that considerate? A man who clearly knew what he wanted and would not let a little thing like somebody else's conflicting desires get in the way?

As she sank into one of the inviting armchairs, Dominique watched Cristiano take up residence at the end of the sofa nearest to her—which was far too close for comfort, if she was honest—and she swallowed hard.

'Yes, it is cold.'

'I can see that you are somewhat tense about this meeting, Dominique. I want to reassure you that I have asked you here only because I want the very best for you and your daughter.'

'That's all well and good, but I'm a little tired of everybody else being convinced they know what's best for me and Matilde!' she snapped, feeling her throat threatening to close.

'How old are you?'

'Twenty-one... Why? I suppose now you're going to tell me that I'm far too young and irresponsible to possibly know my own mind? Well, for your information I know *exactly* what I want for me and my baby, and I don't need anyone else to tell me different!'

A knock on the door heralded the arrival of their coffee and prevented Cristiano from immediately replying to her tirade. While the smartly attired steward arranged an exquisite silver tray on the low burnished wood table in front of them, Dominique tried hard to get her emotions back under control. *Why did the man get to her this way? Make her feel so defensive and angry?*

Watching him tip the steward at the door, she waited until he returned to his seat before she spoke again. 'I'm sorry—I lost my temper.'

'It is an emotional time for all of us. Let me pour you some coffee. Do you take cream and sugar?'

'Yes, please.'

He looked frighteningly calm and collected in comparison with the riot of nerves and emotions she was personally experiencing inside, and as Dominique accepted her drink, his gaze met and held hers for perturbing seconds.

'I spoke to my family last night and I explained to them why you are reticent about returning to Spain with me. They understand your concerns about your job, but—like me—do not see it as an obstacle that cannot be easily overcome. They have implored me to do my utmost to persuade you to come and join us for Christmas at least. You have had some time to think things over and now I would really like your answer, Dominique. What do you say?'

CHAPTER THREE

NO PRESSURE, then...

'I'm still unsure,' she replied. 'They've already organised the rota at the restaurant, and I've promised I'll work.'

'And, apart from working, how were you planning on spending the rest of the holiday?' Cristiano asked quietly.

The question was apt to make her burst into tears. Biting her lip, Dominique covered her distress by briefly raising her cup to her lips and carefully sipping at her drink. 'I was just going to spend it quietly with Matilde.'

'You were not planning on spending any time with your mother?'

Dominique tensed even more. 'She's going skiing with friends, like she always does at Christmas. I probably wouldn't have seen her anyway.'

Cristiano stared at Dominique in disbelief. *Her*

mother was going away with friends, leaving her daughter and grandchild to spend the Christmas holidays entirely alone? He understood that other cultures had different ways of doing things, but this was surely one of the most unnatural things he had ever heard!

Although offended on Dominique's and the baby's behalf, he quickly saw an opportunity for making his case even more compelling, and did not hesitate to take it.

'Christmas where I come from is a truly magical season,' he intoned softly, the edges of his lips lifting in genuine pleasure at the thought. 'At the centre of the tradition is the *belén*—what you call here the Nativity. The scene is recreated using all kinds of lovingly collected materials and passed down through each family, generation to generation. It is something we take great pride in. Sometimes whole communities get together to make the *belén*, and you will find them in many public places as well as in the churches. On Christmas Eve—what we call Nochebuena—the church bells sound joyfully, calling everyone to mass, and afterwards we all return home for a fantastic feast. When that is over we gather round the Christmas tree to sing carols. It is a time for warmth and community…not a time to be alone!'

Dominique's big blue eyes were round with

wonder. Gratified, Cristiano could see that he'd captivated her with the inviting picture his words had conjured up.

'My mother has never believed in making a big fuss at Christmas,' she sighed, her slender shoulders drooping a little in the plain black dress. 'In fact she's always dreaded it rather than looked forward to it. A "commercial rip-off", she calls it. That's why she prefers to go away rather than stay at home.'

'Your mother has her view on the matter and I have mine. But one thing is for certain…you and the little one cannot spend Christmas alone. Consuela would be beside herself if she heard such a thing!'

'Consuela?'

'Ramón's mother.' Cristiano leant towards her, renewed determination in his heart as he thought of the aunt he loved and adored as much as his own mother. 'Come back with me to Spain, Dominique. You will not regret it, I promise.'

'You mean for Christmas? What about my job at the restaurant? I might lose it if I don't work.'

He shook his head impatiently. 'If it comes to it, I will ensure it will not be a problem. I told you…from now on I see it as *my* duty and responsibility to provide for you, and instead of worrying about how to make ends meet if you stay in the UK you will be able to concentrate on the most important job of all in Spain…that of raising your child.'

'And if I decide to accept your offer and stay… what about your own immediate family?' she asked him reasonably. 'Do you have a wife and children? If so, won't they mind you inviting a complete stranger and her baby into your home?'

His body tensing, Cristiano waited for the inevitable feeling of sorrow and regret that pierced him to subside a little. The symptoms were like an illness that persisted, as raw as they had ever been, and he suspected he would *never* be free of them.

'I have neither wife nor child,' he replied, his jaw tightening. 'So the problem would hardly arise. In any case, I am head of the Cordova family and I am entrusted to make decisions that are best for all.'

'You mean…whatever you say goes?'

'If you want to put it like that…yes.'

'I see.'

'Was there anything else you wanted to know?'

She pursed her lips and gazed straight ahead of her. Cristiano's brow furrowed. 'Dominique?'

'It's just that… Well, is it right that I should contemplate going to live with Ramón's family under the circumstances? I mean, when we'd already broken up and everything? It might have been different if we had been engaged to be married, but we weren't.'

'Did you *want* to marry him?'

'No. That was something I never fooled myself about. Even when he was with me he never stopped admiring other girls. I was well aware he craved his freedom and detested the idea of a long-term commitment. A marriage between us wouldn't have lasted five minutes!"

'That may unfortunately have been the case, but I have to tell you that you have *every* right to expect the support of his family, Dominique. It is Matilde's birthright we are talking about here! As well as my own responsibility towards her, Ramón had money and property that will naturally go to his daughter now that he is dead. Once you are established in Spain everything will be arranged legally.'

'Assuming I agree to go, of course!'

Assessing the proud lift of her head and the continued defiance etched into her small, perfect jaw, Cristiano could not help but smile. Victory was close, he sensed, but he would not risk jeopardising it by displaying arrogance at such a crucial juncture.

'I understand your concerns—it is unknown territory for you, and your fears about going to people you do not yet know are only natural. But you are an intelligent girl, and I think you are already aware that returning to Spain with me and the opportunities that would afford you if you decide to stay—as well as the family support you would receive—would surely make for a much better future than you could ever hope to enjoy here!'

She glanced away from him for a moment,

chewing on her lip, her gaze reflective. 'It's a big step…moving to another country. All right. I'll agree to go with you for Christmas, but after that… well, we'll see. My main concern is that I make the right choices for my child. Naturally I want her to be with people who'll love her as much as I do. And I'm well aware she probably won't have that if I stay here. My mother is too bitter and disappointed in me to ever be the kind of grandmother I would wish for Matilde…I realise that.'

'That is *her* loss—of that I have no doubt.'

Equal parts of anger and dismay clutched at Cristiano's vitals when he thought about Dominique's mother and her unforgiving, unnatural attitude towards her daughter. But he was also eager to ring home and give them some good news for a change. To let them know that Dominique and the baby *would* be coming back with him for Christmas would fill them with joy instead of the numbing sadness and grief they had been living with these past few weeks. A baby in the house would signify new life and a new beginning. *New hope.*

The thought laid a soft blanket over his own grief and despair, and he glanced at Dominique with genuine concern, seeing a young woman who clearly needed his protection and guidance. He could not let her down.

'When can you be ready to leave?' he asked her,

stirring his coffee and taking a satisfying sip of the dark sweet brew.

Her cup rattling a little in its saucer as she placed it on the table, Dominique sank further back into her chair and folded her arms. 'Well... I'll have to discuss it with my manager at work, but I'd say the earliest I could go would be in about two weeks' time. If I'm not going to be there over Christmas I'll probably have to put in some extra hours to make up for my absence. There'll be other things to arrange too...a medical check for Matilde, packing, and I'll have to ask my neighbour to keep an eye on my place for me while I'm away.'

'Two weeks is out of the question! I aim to be back in Spain in no more than a week, and I am not going back without you! You can arrange the little one's medical check, but as for your work—I will be only too happy to speak to your manager and put him in the picture. You should be entitled to compassionate leave at the very least!'

Once again Dominique was made aware of the iron resolve of the man sitting opposite her. She recognised his natural proclivity for taking charge of both situations and people—and could not help feeling resentful. She had had a bellyful of being told what to do! Her teachers, her mother... everyone pushing and prodding her to achieve their *own* ends, not hers. If she was going to become part of this new Spanish family that her daughter had inherited then she had to establish for Cristiano Cordova the fact that she had a mind and a will of her own, and would not be backed into a corner by anyone.

'That won't be necessary. I'm quite capable of speaking to my manager myself, thank you! And if you can't wait as long as two weeks, then why don't you go back as planned and let me follow on later?'

'No.'

Dominique had never heard such an intractable no in her life. Getting to his feet, Cristiano appeared suddenly restless, as if he had sat too long and was unused to such enforced inactivity.

'We will return to Spain together and I will not hear of any other arrangement than that! Over the coming week I will be totally at your disposal to help you with whatever has to be done—and it will be done, rest assured. And, talking of travelling, you have an up-to-date passport, I presume?'

Dominique nodded, her expression stunned.

'And Matilde?'

'Well, no,' Dominique answered. 'There's hardly been a need…'

'No matter—I can easily speed things up with a word in the right ear at the embassy. And as for packing—you will not need to bring much with you when you first come out at all. I will ensure absolutely everything you need will be provided once we arrive back home.'

'Can you turn water into wine too?'

He stared at her with a dark look in his eyes.

'Very amusing! I can see that it will take time for you to become used to how I operate, Dominique, but you will soon learn. When I say a thing should be done then it is done without question, and I want you to know that I will be completely unrelenting in my goal to have Ramón's daughter *and* her mother on Spanish soil sooner rather than later. I am absolutely adamant about that!'

Her cheeks twin beacons of indignant scarlet at his words, Dominique stubbornly refused to shy away from Cristiano's arrogant gaze. But an icy chill of warning slid down her spine. *Ramón had been right...his cousin was, indeed, formidable.*

'And I want *you* to know that whilst I may be young I'm no badly behaved five-year-old who needs to be told what to do—so don't treat me like I am!'

'Is that so? I will endeavour to try and remember that. I am beginning to see that Ramón certainly had his work cut out for him being with you, Dominique!'

To Dominique's complete surprise, Cristiano's steely-eyed glare was swiftly replaced by a teasing glance that made heat erupt inside her like a rip tide, scorching right through her centre.

Stunned by her disturbing response—and suddenly not feeling quite so defiant—she pushed to her feet. 'I need to use the bathroom,' she mumbled and, disconcerted that the smile had still not completely left her tormentor's lips, she hurried away in the direction he indicated.

Standing in the luxurious marble bathroom, in front of a huge antique mirror edged with gold-painted rosebuds and curlicues, Dominique surveyed her flushed, heated face with impatience and surprise. *What had just happened in there?* Why was the man getting to her so? Dropping her shoulders, she flicked her hair back over her shoulder and sighed. She was scared, that was all. Fear was apt to make her anxious and edgy, liable to react nervously to even the most inconsequential thing.

But how could she feel anything *but* scared about the possibility of going to live in Spain amongst people she didn't know, as well as putting herself under the daunting wing of a man like Cristiano Cordova? It hardly surprised her that he was a lawyer—no doubt a frighteningly successful one too. Once they were in his sphere, he would hold her and Matilde's futures in his hands as ruthlessly and single-mindedly as he controlled the fates of the people he represented in court, she was sure.

Yet, even so, Dominique realised that this was

the right thing to do for her child. She might not have had the chance to find out about her own father, or be close to his family, but Matilde *would*. And even though she could foresee that sparks would fly between herself and Cristiano—he would want to control her and Dominique would naturally want to resist being manipulated in any way—he had told her that his family were kind, loving people, and the picture he had painted so evocatively of the kind of Christmases they enjoyed had been compelling. Her heart had squeezed with longing for such an experience.

If only she could trust what he said, then maybe she could start to allow herself to hope that the future might not be so frightening as she feared. She *ached* to feel connected to the rest of the world again…not to be cut off by people who were so emotionally distant that they made Dominique feel like an island in a stark, cold sea. Her mother had scorned her for throwing away her future by having Matilde, but it was her emotional neglect that had driven her into Ramón Cordova's arms in the first place.

Ramón. Even though he had been thoughtless and wild, and in the end had rejected her, when they'd been together he had given her more attention and affection than anyone else ever had. He had shown her what it was to laugh too, to be young and foolish and not to take life so seriously.

Suddenly it hit her hard that he was dead—his vibrant young life ended before it had really begun, leaving his child without even the possibility of ever meeting him. She felt her whole body sag towards the floor, as if some strange irresistible force were dragging her down, down into a dark abyss, and tears welled up in her eyes like hot springs, rolling down her cheeks in glistening wet tracks. *Was she destined to be alone and unloved for ever?* She almost couldn't bear it.

'Dominique? Is everything all right?'

Cristiano's voice sounded from the other side of the door. Straightening in shock, Dominique ripped a tissue out of the chic box on the vanity unit, blew her nose and mumbled, 'I'm fine. I just need a minute, okay?'

'You are crying,' he retorted, his voice accusing.

'I suppose that's a hanging offence where you come from?' she burst out, unable to help herself.

'Do not be so foolish! I never said it was an offence to cry.'

There was a surprisingly gentle quality to his tone that Dominique had not heard before.

'But if you are upset I would like to help comfort you,' he added.

Comfort… Spiritual, emotional, physical… It was the thing she longed for, but somehow it always escaped her. The distressing events of the past year had all but ripped away her confidence and trust in everything, and on top of that her hormones were going haywire after having Matilde.

'You are the *last* person I would want to comfort me!' she heard herself rail, before she could stem the impulse.

There was silence outside for a long moment, then Cristiano spoke again, his voice low and his words measured.

'Maybe you would prefer it if it was my cousin standing outside this door talking to you? But as we both know that is not possible. You will simply have to make do with me. Open the door, Dominique.'

'I don't want Ramón!' she answered, her tears coming faster. 'Why would I want him? It was over between us a long time ago, and he walked out on me—remember? It's just such a waste, that's all—to die like that! A stupid, *stupid* waste!'

Glancing at her stricken expression sidelong in the mirror, Dominique gulped down another sob and dabbed feverishly at her reddened eyes.

'Sometimes it is hard to make sense of these things, even when one has faith… But life goes on, yes? And you have a beautiful baby daughter to remember him by. Not all is lost.'

Strangely comforted by his words, Dominique took a deep breath, then shakily released the latch and opened the door. The handsome visage that confronted her was both grave and concerned, and she didn't know why she should feel so guilty about yelling at him, but she did. He was, after all, throwing her a lifeline of sorts, as well as giving Matilde an opportunity to grow up knowing the family that had raised her father…

'There is a park close by,' Cristiano told her, dark eyes assessing her tear-stained face with intimate scrutiny. 'The day is bright and cold—I think we should take a walk together and get some air. What do you say?'

'I don't know. Yes…all right.' But even as she agreed, Dominique sensed her lip quiver uncontrollably and her face crumple. 'I'm just so *tired*!' she breathed mournfully, dipping her head. 'So tired of everything!'

In the next instant Cristiano had propelled her into his arms and was cradling her head against his chest, just over his heart. The steady, even throb of his heartbeat and the comforting sensation of warmth and strength that emanated from his hard, masculine body made Dominique curl her fingers into his fine wool sweater for added security, and she gratefully shut her eyes, feeling as if they stood together in the eye of a storm. She prayed it would soon pass. But her scalding tears would not be so easily contained, and they seeped from her eyelids in a steady trickle of pain and sorrow. *What was the matter with her?* After all this time of staying strong, telling herself she could cope come what may, she was suddenly falling apart.

'Cry all you want, *querida,*' the man who held her murmured in his compelling velvet-lined voice, his big hand cupping her head and stroking her hair as though tenderly giving consolation to a child. 'Expressing our sorrows is sometimes necessary rather then holding them inside. You should not see giving in to grief as something undesirable, or feel that you have to put on a brave face when you are feeling sad. That would not be good for you *or* the little one!'

For disturbing moments Cristiano felt as if his feelings were under siege as he held Dominique's slender quivering body close to his own. The scent of her honey-laced shampoo was inexplicably alluring as it drifted beneath his nose, and he had never touched hair of such fine silk as hers before. The sensation was *incredible*. He was aware too of the soft fullness of her breasts as they pressed intimately into his chest, and was shocked by the entirely inappropriate sensations that swept violently through his body as a result of that close contact.

It had been too long since he had held a woman in his arms, and no doubt *that* was why his body was reacting so strongly. All he had wanted to do was offer Dominique some comfort and reassurance, but now her body was awakening feelings in him that he'd thought long petrified. If the sensations were purely sexual he could handle them well enough—women had always been interested in Cristiano, and there had been no lack of opportunity for that kind of consolation since the tragedy that had stopped his world. But other, much more *dangerous* emotions were assailing him too, and Cristiano realised he would have to be on his guard against getting this close to the beguiling Dominique again. The risks were simply too terrifying to be contemplated…

CHAPTER FOUR

AS HER tears and sorrow started to abate, Dominique became disturbingly aware that she was actively *enjoying* being held in Cristiano's arms. Not just because he was giving her the comfort she sorely needed, but because his body was hard and warm and strong, and the contact made her feel *alive* and human again, after being shut off from those vital sensations for too long.

Now she knew why babies failed to thrive when they were denied the most basic necessity of all...that of being touched and held. Surely something similar must happen to adults? And it was with genuine reluctance that she uncurled her fingers from the soft weave of Cristiano's sweater and started to step out of the protective circle of his arms.

Just before Dominique disengaged herself completely, he took her hands in his and stroked the pads of his thumbs back and forth across her fine, delicately boned fingers. His dark gaze was almost brooding.

'It will get better, you know? You will find a way to manage it. I know it is hard to believe that right now, feeling the way you do, but you will. Every day the hurt will ease a little more. You are fortunate that you have little Matilde to draw comfort from.'

He sounded as if he knew intimately what it was to lose someone you cared for. Staring back into the black velvet night of his arresting glance, Dominique felt her hands alive with electricity from their contact with his. Her grief and despondency had been stunningly transformed into a fascination that perplexed and frightened her.

'I think I'll give that walk a miss, if you don't mind? I really ought to be getting back to Matilde,' she heard herself announce, her voice sounding remarkably even and calm in spite of her turbulent feelings.

Cristiano shrugged, his expression not easing in its disturbing intensity one iota. 'When can I see you again?' he asked.

Her heart momentarily stalled at the question—*for a second there he had sounded like an ardent lover, counting the minutes until he saw his paramour again*—and Dominique sensed heat rush into her face.

'Why don't you come and join me for dinner

this evening? You can bring the baby...I will see about a private room for us,' he suggested when she did not reply straight away.

'I can't. I'm working tonight.'

'Ring them and say that you are taking the night off.'

'Are solutions always so black and white to you?'

Dominique bet when this man dealt with clients he didn't suffer fools gladly, or grant any quarter to anyone who dared disagree with him. The world must seem a very different place when you saw the answers to problems with such enviable clarity!

'I'm already going to have to let them down when I tell them I can't work over Christmas as it is. It would hardly be fair for me to phone in at the last minute and say I'm taking tonight off as well!'

'I can see that you have a very admirable sense of duty, Dominique, and although I am disappointed you won't be joining me tonight I cannot fault it. So... We will meet tomorrow for lunch instead, yes? We can go for a walk in the park first, then have something to eat afterwards. Does that plan appeal more to your sense of fairness?'

His lips twitched teasingly upwards at one corner, and Dominique was transfixed by the blaze of light that humour brought to his otherwise smouldering dark gaze.

'It does.'

'So…if you insist you have to leave now I will ring down to Reception and organise a car to take you back home. I will send it again for you tomorrow at around midday.'

'Okay…thank you.'

'You are feeling a little better now?'

As he brought his hand lightly down onto her shoulder, Cristiano's touch almost made Dominique jump out of her skin.

'I'm sorry I lost it like that.' She grimaced, hardly daring to look at him and suddenly needing vital fresh air to help her breathe.

'There is no need for an apology,' he said quietly, devastatingly holding her gaze, even though everything inside her was clamouring to be set free from it.

When she could hardly stand the tension any longer, he gave a barely perceptible nod of his head and moved towards the telephone on the bureau just inside the door. Seconds later she heard him ring down to Reception to order the car to take her home…

Having spoken to his family and given them the news that they'd been waiting on tenterhooks to hear, Cristiano strode restlessly through the hotel and made his way to the park. As he slid his ungloved hands into the pockets of his camel-coloured cashmere coat and made his way down paths strewn with the untended debris of faded and dead autumn leaves his thoughts turned like a magnet to Dominique and the baby.

Both females were stirring things in him that he had rigidly striven to keep contained—an action that stemmed from his great desire to make himself impenetrable to hurt from another human being again. Up until Ramón's shocking death he had more than succeeded. But now the big blue guile-less eyes of the woman his cousin had abandoned, along with her fierce pride and that gorgeous baby girl, were making inroads into the previously imper-vious wall he'd built around his emotions. He knew he would have to fortify it if he was to stay immune.

He didn't doubt for a moment that he was doing the right thing in taking them home with him to Spain—his sense of duty and familial loyalty con-firmed it, if nothing else—nevertheless Cristiano knew that their unexpected presence in his life was going to test his resolve as nothing had before.

As he sighed into the frigid air, his warm breath made a curling plume of steam. A well-dressed couple strolling past from the opposite direction wished him good afternoon, and Cristiano politely inclined his head in acknowledgement. As he walked on, he was blindsided as his mind's eye caught and held the vision of another woman's beautiful face. The pain it wrought inside him almost made him stagger.

Unable to fight off the scene that unfolded in his head, he devastatingly recalled the passionate, loving words that woman had called out to him from her hospital bed just two years ago. A seemingly straight forward labour had taken an unexpected turn for the worse, and the next thing Cristiano had known was that his wife was fighting for her life—and their baby's. Just before the medical team had rushed her off to surgery Martina had called out to him. *'Te amo, Cristi! Te amo!'* Her stunning brown eyes had been full of tears and so had his own as he'd stood there, icy dread robbing him of all life and turning him to stone, nauseous with the realisation that he was in the middle of a nightmare he might never wake from…

All his faith, personal influence, professional know-how and wealth had served him to no avail that terrible day, and by the time he'd received the news that his wife and baby had not survived the emergency operation that had been undertaken to save them Cristiano had felt as if he had been driven to his knees by the most vicious, merciless storm imaginable.

The pain of it was as fresh now as it had been that day, despite the platitudes he had spoken earlier. Gritting his teeth, he lengthened his stride and began to head down a path that he saw led to a large wintry lake flocked by squawking birds, and with a determined upsurge of strength he managed to ride the crest of the terrible emotion that had so cruelly racked him. Eventually sensing it subside, he renewed his vow never to leave himself so vulnerable again.

Knowing they were going to the park, Dominique had hoped they would go by the lake, so she'd brought with her a paper bag full of stale crusts of bread to feed to the birds. Cristiano seemed quite happy to go along with this idea and, despite being dressed more appropriately for lunch at the Ritz than to take a casual stroll through the park, he walked alongside Matilde's pushchair closely enough to look as if he belonged there. It gave Dominique quite an odd feeling. And even odder was the fact that she realised she couldn't really imagine Ramón undertaking the same ordinary action and taking pleasure in it. He would have been too impatient to go on and do something far more exciting, and would probably have spoiled the outing with a sulk.

Guiltily Dominique pulled herself up short. *Was she being disloyal to the father of her baby by thinking such an uncharitable thing?* Disturbed, she pushed the thought away and glanced sidelong at Cristiano instead. This morning she'd woken with a strange fluttering sensation in the pit of her stomach and had realised it was excitement at the idea of going to Spain. Somehow this man walking beside her had persuaded her it would be a very good idea for her to go, and for some reason Dominique had started to believe him.

Whether it was the thought of spending a Christmas like the one he had so vividly described, amongst people who genuinely cared about her daughter's wellbeing, or just the opportunity to consider starting life afresh in a new country with a 'clean slate,' she couldn't have said for sure, but she knew she had to give it a try. There was certainly nothing holding her in the UK if she decided to move there permanently, and that included her mother. Talking of which…

'By the way, I spoke to my mother this morning and told her I was going to Spain with you for Christmas.'

'And how did she take the news?'

'She was strangely quiet, actually. Not the reaction I expected at all. She said we should talk when I get back.'

'Perhaps she has finally realised how selfish of her it is to leave you to your own devices during the holiday?'

'Why should she think that?' Shrugging, Dominique countered the sting of her mother's rejection of both her and her baby with a fresh spurt of anger. 'It's what she usually does! It would be a bit late in the day for her to develop a conscience!'

'You have never mentioned your father?' Interestedly, Cristiano glanced at her. 'I am presuming he is not in the picture any more?'

'He left when I was two. God knows where he is now! He never kept in touch, and I doubt whether my mother would have even wanted him to. She's been furious with him for most of my life! It's her main motivation for getting up every day…just so she can be mad at him all over again!'

Not commenting, Cristiano merely looked thoughtful, and Dominique concluded that he was obviously thinking what a screwed up family she came from!

Biting her lip, she tightened her hands a little round the handlebars of the pushchair.

Reaching the lakeside, Dominique carefully positioned Matilde where she had the best view and, checking that the cheerful knitted blanket to safeguard her from the cold was securely in place, she crouched down low beside her and laughingly threw the crusts to the accumulated feathered throng.

'Look, Tilly! Look at the lovely birds, darling! How happy they are to see you!'

Watching them both with growing fascination, and a secret pleasure he could not deny, Cristiano stood protectively by, his gaze moving now and again to the other small groups of families dotted round the perimeter of the lake, also feeding the birds. His connection to the young woman beside him was for once allowing him entry to an experience that they perhaps took for granted. He valiantly steered his mind away from the distressing recollection that had assailed him yesterday and concentrated instead on this new memory that Dominique and her sweet child were helping to create.

'Make yourself useful!' she chided him suddenly, passing him a handful of crusts and gazing up at him with teasing mirth in her brilliant blue eyes. 'I've literally got enough here to feed the five thousand!'

'If you ask me' Cristiano responded drolly, 'those birds already look overfed. Any more food and they will not be able to take off!'

'A sense of humour, Señor Cordova? I didn't expect that!'

'You think I am too serious?' he asked, frowning, not quite knowing how to take her criticism.

'Perhaps...I don't really know. It's just that you seemed like you were miles away, that's all.'

'I was merely observing the other people doing what you are doing and wondering how it is that a simple pastime such as throwing some bread to birds can bring so much pleasure.'

'When you do it with your children it's the best thing in the world!' Dominique announced, leaning into Matilde's pushchair to plant a sound kiss on her daughter's plump pink cheek. 'Isn't it, Tilly?'

Cristiano remained silent in bittersweet agreement, but as his gaze locked with Dominique's a palpable sensation of warmth seemed to flood his insides. His previous disquiet vanished and he knew he was staring. The icy wind that was blowing had stung her cheeks into two bright pink spots of colour, and some fine strands of honey-brown hair, freed from her plait, danced wildly across them.

She glanced quickly away, clearly discomfited by his intense regard. 'When we've got rid of all the bread, do you think we could go and eat?' she asked him, her gaze now firmly on the lake and the diving birds as they braved the near-frozen surface to reach the semi-submerged crusts.

Concerned that he had neglected his duties, Cristiano agreed straight away. 'Of course! Do you like Indian food?' he asked her. 'There is an exceptionally good Indian restaurant nearby, where I have reserved a table for us. If you do not like that particular cuisine then we can go somewhere you'd like better.'

'Indian is great…as long as you think I'm dressed okay? It's not somewhere really posh, is it?'

'No…it is not "posh".' His lips curved into an amused smile. 'It has an authentic Indian ambience, and you can go dressed casually—as we are.'

'What you're wearing is *casual?*' Now it was Dominique's turn to be amused.

Glancing down at his smart chinos, handmade Italian shoes, black cashmere sweater and three-quarter-length black leather jacket, Cristiano was genuinely perplexed by the question. 'My outfit is certainly not formal, if that is what you are suggesting!'

'No…perhaps it isn't formal, but it still looks expensive and classy. Whereas what I'm wearing definitely doesn't! Perhaps we ought to just go for a burger somewhere? I don't want to embarrass you.'

She was wearing denim jeans, boots, a bottle-green polo-necked sweater and the slightly over-sized tweed coat she'd had on yesterday. Very little make-up adorned her features, and she looked fresh-faced, young and beautiful. Why she imagined he would be *remotely* embarrassed to be seen with her appearing as she was Cristiano could not begin to fathom. He did not like the sense that her parents' emotional neglect of her—as well as his cousin's abandonment—had made such a harsh dent in her self-esteem.

'That is an entirely ridiculous notion, Dominique! You look perfectly acceptable to me. All I want you to do is enjoy the food and hopefully the company too.' He smiled wryly. 'Put your worries aside for a while.'

'And they won't mind at the restaurant if I feed the baby while I'm there?'

'You are feeding her yourself?' For a moment Cristiano sensed an intense tingling heat throb low in his stomach at the idea of Dominique breastfeeding, and he was furious with himself for feeling aroused when it was the most natural thing in the world for a mother to feed her baby that way. He noticed the colour in her cheeks bloomed even pinker at his question.

'No. I tried to feed her myself but I had to give up in the end. I wasn't very good at it.'

'But she takes a bottle quite happily?'

Dominique nodded.

'Then where is the problem? As long as she is able to take nourishment that is the main thing, is it not?'

Glancing towards the lake, Cristiano threw a handful of bread in the direction of a rather dejected-looking duck that was isolated from the rest, He shivered as a particularly icy breeze seared into his face just then. As pleasurable as this little outing with Dominique and the baby was, he was seriously missing the far friendlier climes of his own country. He was also concerned that it was too much for the child to be out in such hostile weather.

'We should go now,' he announced, swiping the remainder of the crumbs from his leather gloves. 'It is really far too bitter for Matilde. We should get her inside into the warmth.'

'You're probably right. Say bye-bye to the birds, Tilly! We'll come and visit them again another day.'

Rising to her feet, Dominique gave Cristiano a fleeting smile, and as she turned the pushchair round and started back up the path that had led them to the lake he automatically put his hand at her back, as if to guide and protect her...

CHAPTER FIVE

IT WAS going to be the last night Dominique spent in her bedsit for a while—at least until after Christmas, and maybe longer than that if she decided to take the monumental step of settling in Spain. She'd had a farewell drink with a couple of close friends, and Katie from across the landing, and now all she had to do was finish her packing. Thankfully Matilde was being an absolute angel and sleeping peacefully—tired out, Dominique was sure, from being cuddled and petted by the three girls who'd dropped in to say goodbye to them.

Tomorrow was the big day. She and Matilde were flying out to Madrid with Cristiano, and when they arrived his personal driver was going to meet them and transport them the seventy kilometres to the town where he lived. The thought was exciting, but somewhat overwhelming too. Cristiano kept telling her not to be daunted—that everything would work out perfectly—but Dominique could not help fearing it might not, and then where would she be? Back in this too-small bedsit with a growing infant and barely enough money coming in to make ends meet.

Pausing as she turned to the half-filled suitcase she'd hefted onto the foldaway bed that doubled up as a couch during the day, Dominique sighed heavily as she gazed critically round her. As optimistic as she'd tried to be when she'd first set eyes on the place, she'd be a liar if she didn't admit the rundown décor and general living conditions weren't depressing. If she hadn't had a baby to look after and a job to go to five nights a week perhaps she might have got round to doing some redecoration to freshen it up a little…

No…she was glad to be leaving this bleak, dreary environment to go somewhere warmer and more welcoming. The only thing that was really making her stomach roll over time and time again was the idea of going with Cristiano. Seeing him on and off over the past few days, for lunch or coffee, and walks in the park whenever she could grab an hour or two away from the demands of her week, had not lessened her heightened awareness of the man one jot. She had learned that he definitely liked to take charge, that he had certain old-fashioned views about men taking care of women, and that he could be brusque one minute then absolutely charming the next. With Matilde he'd assumed the role of a very fond uncle, and he loved to make a fuss of her and buy her little gifts—pretty dresses and baby toys that had clearly been purchased from the more upmarket department stores.

All in all, he did the things that most women would love their children's fathers to do for them, and Dominique sensed that her vow to distance herself from men in general after what had happened with Ramón was being seriously compromised by his appealing attentions. However, she knew that once back in Spain Cristiano would have his own very independent life to lead, and although he would be close at hand, she and Matilde would not command his attention half so much as they did here.

That was good, she told herself. She absolutely did not want to need or depend on him— She had learned too well how no one could be relied upon. But it would be very hard when she had become so used to his presence as well as his reassurance and advice. Somewhere deep inside Dominique sensed a warning that she knew she should seriously heed. She'd already been abandoned by her father, and the father of her child. Did she want to risk making the same catastrophic mistake again by becoming too attached to Cristiano? He was merely acting as a sort of guardian for her and Matilde until he got them safely back to Spain, and that was all. After that his life would resume as normal, and Dominique would be busy getting used to a completely new situation—as well as a whole new set of people on her own. The thought gave her serious butterflies.

The phone rang, startling her, and she scrubbed a hand round her face to help focus. Her tone had an unknowingly husky cadence as she spoke into the receiver. 'Hello?'

'Dominique?'

The sensually commanding Spanish voice that answered had become compellingly familiar, and an involuntary shiver rushed through her at the sound of it.

'I was wondering if you might ring,' she replied, shocked that the word she had actually been going to use was *hoping*. Feeling mild irritation at her foolishness, she was glad that Cristiano wasn't there in person to witness her telling blush.

'How is the packing coming along?' he asked, and she heard the smile in his voice.

Glancing down at the only half-full suitcase, Dominique grimaced. 'Actually, I had to take a break from it for a while. I had some friends round this evening to wish me bon voyage, and I've only just got Matilde off to sleep after all the excitement. I'm just about to carry on.'

'Do you need any help? I could be there in about half an hour.'

'No! There really isn't any need…thanks.'

Her hand was shaking as she threaded it through her hair. Right now she didn't need the added distraction of his presence, and besides, she was sure he had seen enough of her depressing bedsit. No, she would be far more relaxed packing her meagre belongings on her own rather than have Cristiano helping her.

'It won't take me long, and then when I'm done I'm going straight to bed. We have an early start in the morning, right?'

'I will be there to collect you at around eight-thirty. Our flight is at eleven. I hope the baby won't disturb you too much tonight…you will need your rest with all the travelling we have ahead of us.'

'I have a feeling she'll sleep through.'

'Good. I rang my family earlier, and they will definitely *not* be sleeping through,' he said ironically. 'They are overwhelmed at the idea that you are coming and they are going to see Ramón's daughter at last.'

'No more overwhelmed than I am at the thought of meeting *them*.'

'You have nothing to worry about.'

'So you keep telling me!'

'And what I am telling you is the truth. Anyway…I

think I should let you go now and finish your packing. *Buenas noches*, Dominique. Sleep well.'

'Goodnight…'

Suddenly saying his name seemed too intimate, so she chose to exclude it, but as she replaced the receiver on its rest it came to her that she was holding her breath…

Matilde had won over the airline staff as soon as they boarded, and during the flight in the first class cabin the steward and stewardess assigned to look after them took every opportunity to stop and make a fuss of the beautiful infant. In turn, her huge brown eyes and happy dimpled smile declared her definite approval of being the centre of so much attention.

Cristiano could not help but feel a strong wave of pride that the irresistible little girl had Cordova blood running in her veins, and he knew that when she was grown she would be a *magnet* for all the young men in the vicinity. He frowned, surprised by the worry this thought produced. Already protective towards her, he also sensed a definite possessiveness where her mother was concerned, and that perturbed him. Dominique was young and beautiful. Some day she would marry, and another man would assume the role of guardian and protector to her and her child. *And that was just as it should be.* Cristiano would be relegated to a far less important role in their lives and he would simply have to learn to accept it. His jaw tightened.

Glancing at Dominique now, as she stared out of the window at the clouds—just as he himself had been doing only a week ago on his way to meet her—he silently observed her classic, flawless profile and knew great pleasure in doing so. Matilde had fallen asleep on her lap, and the baby's head was snuggled into the groove of her arm. Together they made the most beguiling tableau.

'What do you see out there amongst the clouds?' he asked softly, leaning towards her.

Her dreamy blue-eyed gaze settled on his face in surprise. 'It's compelling, isn't it? It makes me wish I could fly…get away from everything troubling that's going on down there on the ground and escape up here into the silence and solitude. That would be amazing!'

A frisson of concern rippled through Cristiano. 'This world makes you wish to escape it?'

'Doesn't everybody feel like that from time to time? What's the matter? Have I said something wrong?'

'No. Of course not.' Determinedly releasing the tension that had gathered between his shoulderblades, Cristiano put aside the distressing notion concerning his cousin's death that sometimes plagued his mind and focused on the lovely face before him instead. 'It is just that I want you to know that you have everything to live for, Dominique. Life has been a challenge sometimes, yes…but now you are coming to Spain it will get much easier for you…trust me.'

'I do. I have to—or else I wouldn't have come, would I?' Her glance was brief but intense.

As she pulled her gaze away Cristiano almost wanted to command her to look back again. He touched her arm. 'You look tired,' he observed. 'Give me the little one and take a nap for a while.'

'Are you sure?'

'Of course.'

Carefully Dominique lifted the still sleeping Matilde into his arms and, feeling the slight but warm and pliable weight of the infant sag against him, Cristiano was again struck by how protective he felt towards the child. Settling back into his padded reclining seat with the baby held firmly against his chest, he sensed the kind of peace that he had not experienced in a very long while steal over him. And the truth was he found it almost too seductive for words…

The impressive edifice loomed up before Dominique like some intimidating Moorish citadel from the ancient past, and her blue eyes widened in surprise. When she'd thought about what Cristiano's home might be like she hadn't really known what to expect, and hadn't asked. But in her wildest dreams she would never have imagined something on the scale of grandeur and beauty she was seeing now!

Cristiano's driver—who had introduced himself at the airport as Valentín—smoothly drove the luxuriously upholstered black sedan up the twisting walled road that led straight to the entrance, and, craning to see out of the window, Dominique saw three women standing outside in the courtyard, in front of a huge double-fronted doorway. It was coming on to late afternoon, but the sun was still a banner of fierce brightness in the sky and she shielded her gaze with her hand from the stunning glare.

Sensing movement beside her, she turned as Cristiano's depthless sable eyes sought hers. 'We are here. And, as you can see, your eager reception committee is waiting.'

He smiled and there was something else in his glance besides satisfaction in reaching their journey's end that Dominique couldn't readily identify. Something that made her feel as though she was falling, with no glimpse of where or how she would land…

Her stomach turned hollow.

'Gaaa!' Wriggling in her baby seat, a now wide-eyed Matilde reached out to Cristiano with a gummy grin.

Catching the tiny plump hand that waved wildly in the air, he raised it to his lips and kissed it. 'The same to you, my little princess! Now, let us go and see who is waiting to meet you. May I?' he asked Dominique, and when she nodded agreement he carefully lifted the baby into his arms once more.

To tell the truth, Dominique was glad he had offered to take her daughter, because now it came to it she realised just how acutely anxious she really was about this meeting. Out on the gravelled court-yard the sun was still beating down with surprising force for December—and Dominique moved towards the little group that was waiting to greet them with Cristiano and Matilde just ahead of her, her heart galloping and her stomach turning uneasy cartwheels.

She prayed that any impending awkwardness that might surface would soon be behind her, so that she could at least try and relax a little, but her mind was racing with fear and doubt. *What if Ramón's mother believed that Dominique had somehow driven her son away? What if she blamed her or felt resentful that she lived while he had died?* She knew her wild speculation made no sense, but she couldn't seem to help herself.

In the group that was gathered there were two older women and one perhaps a little bit older than Dominique herself, and she saw that one of the older women was wearing black. For Ramón? she speculated. This, then, must be his mother. All the women were strikingly attractive, with the same midnight-dark hair as Cristiano, but in the two older women it was threaded with pure silver.

The woman dressed in black moved towards Cristiano and the baby with tears streaming freely down her face. Most of what followed speech-wise Dominique could not understand, not being familiar yet with the language, but she did hear 'Ramón' and *'la niña'* several times, and the emotion in the other woman's voice acted as a catalyst for her own. She swallowed hard to try and contain it, her heart full to overflowing as she watched the woman who must be Ramón's mother lift a curious-looking Matilde eagerly but lovingly into her arms. Then tears turned quickly to beaming smiles, and the baby was showered with kisses and more loving attention—not just from the woman who held her, but from the other two women as well.

Feeling somewhat redundant, yet strangely happy as she viewed the highly emotional scene, she glanced up in surprise as Cristiano stretched his hand out, indicating she should go to him.

'Dominique…' The pale, slender palm she slid into his was given a reassuring and firm squeeze that sent immediate goosebumps flying across the surface of her skin. 'Come and meet my family. This is my mother, Luisa.'

Warm eyes with the gloss of silky dark chocolate beamed back at her. Then, without further ado, she found herself being kissed soundly on both cheeks and pulled urgently against the other woman's ample bosom for a fierce, affectionate hug.

'Dominique!' she heard, in Luisa's halting, deeply accented voice. 'Words cannot describe what we are all feeling today. The baby—she is…she is so—so important to us, we cannot tell you! Cristiano… Please, my son, explain.'

'In my family,' he began, his dark gaze settling gravely on Dominique, 'my mother and Consuela are the only ones left. They have lost nearly everyone… parents, uncles, aunts…their husbands, of course. I am not married, and neither is my sister Elena. Therefore there were no grandchildren until Matilde. What my mother would like me to convey to you is that she is our hope for the future…and so she is very, very precious to us all.'

Dominique stared—first at Cristiano, then at Luisa, then at Ramón's mother, who was grinning from ear to ear as she jiggled a now laughing Matilde. *So much loss…* It was unbelievable. She was almost unbearably moved. For the first time since Cristiano had suggested it, she felt a sudden clear certainty that she had done absolutely the right thing in coming to Spain, and in that moment she knew she would stay. There was a lot of healing to be done here, and who knew? Perhaps her beloved child would help start the fragile process?

'Well…I'm very pleased to be here with Matilde, Luisa. Even though the circumstances are so sad.'

'You must call me Mamá,' Luisa instructed immediately, grabbing Dominique's hand and patting it. She glanced at her son, watching the proceedings with his usual quiet, dignified gravity. 'She is very beautiful, is she not, Cristiano?'

His pensive glance touched Dominique's for a long, disturbing second. '*Sí.* She is.'

'I am Elena.' The stunning younger brunette stepped away from Ramón's mother's side at that moment and gave her a quick, hard hug.

Her perfume was gorgeous, and no doubt expensive, but there was nothing stand-offish or superior in her manner, and for some reason, Dominique warmed to her right away.

'The baby is so lovely! We are all just so excited to have you with us in time for Christmas, and hopefully after that you will decide to settle here permanently! I am afraid that Consuela's English is not as good as my own, or my mother's, but she so wants to speak with you and I will be happy to translate.'

Addressing the woman who held the still smiling

Matilde so tenderly, Elena indicated she should come closer. Consuela stared deeply into Dominique's anxious gaze and spoke in a passionate, clearly emotional flood of Spanish.

'She says she is honoured to meet the mother of her son's child. She wants me to tell you that although her heart is broken because she has lost her beautiful son, she feels that she has been blessed by the Holy Virgin herself because you had his baby—even though he did not take care of you as he should have. Ramón was not a bad person…only troubled.'

Wary of the lump forming inside her throat, Dominique smiled and nodded to show Consuela that she appreciated what she said. She took a moment before she asked Elena to convey to her that there was no blame in her own heart for what Ramón had done, only a great sadness that he had not lived to see the beautiful daughter he had fathered.

All the while she was speaking, Dominique had been keenly aware of Cristiano listening intently to what was being said, and a big part of her wanted to go to him and lay her head on the broad, hard-muscled shoulder she was fighting so hard not to depend on. Reminding herself that she had to cultivate a distance from him emotionally—*not* get even more deeply involved that way—she leant forward and kissed Consuela affectionately on her cheek.

'*Gracias,*' she said softly. 'Thank you for inviting

me and Matilde to come and stay with you. I honestly was not looking forward to the two of us spending Christmas alone.'

As Elena translated, Cristiano moved closer.

'Let me take you and show you where you will be sleeping.' He put a hand beneath Dominique's elbow, and the expression on his bronzed handsome face was hard to decipher even as he bestowed a warm, tender smile on the other women. 'Consuela, why don't you take care of the little one while I show Dominique to her rooms?' he suggested.

CHAPTER SIX

THE house—if you could call it that—was like its own little kingdom.

Everywhere Dominique looked were soaring stone arches leading into door-lined corridors. But although it was certainly vast, somehow the family that lived there had cultivated a distinctly warm and welcoming ambience inside, instead of one that might so easily have been distant and intimidating because of its sheer dimensions.

There were homely touches everywhere. Family photographs in the most elegant frames sat atop classically designed furniture as well as on more native, unvarnished pieces. Vases of exotic blooms were plentiful, as were vivid and colourful tapestries adorning the thick earthen walls that were securely reinforced by tall brick pillars. Candles abounded, as well as a plethora of bookcases in different cosy alcoves, crammed with books of all kinds—and usually with a comfortable chair nearby, Dominique noticed, in which to sit and read undisturbed. Charmingly, every windowsill also housed a small, simply designed lamp of some kind.

But the thing that arrested her attention the most was the unique flavour of the country and its people that somehow permeated the atmosphere and wrapped itself round her enraptured senses as though casting a spell. Walking through that amazing building, with its mosaic-tiled floors, arabesque design work and compelling artefacts, Dominique had the sense that she was being somehow trans-ported back through time. This might easily have been the palace of a sultan or an emir! An excited shiver ran down her spine. *It was strange…but now that she was here she didn't feel as alien as she'd thought she might.* In fact, she had the oddest sense of belonging that she couldn't explain.

Standing at the entrance to the most exquisite bedroom, after negotiating countless corridors and one grand sweeping staircase with Cristiano, Dominique likened herself to a shipwreck survivor who had somehow, by angelic intervention, been washed up on the shores of a beautiful island filled with every lush fruit known to man. As her brooding escort silently watched her, she was almost too over-whelmed for words by the sight that met her gaze.

The room she viewed was one of the two allocated to her, comprising a sitting room and bedroom, and was the most luxuriously appointed she'd ever contemplated staying in. Drawing the eye immediately was a very grand and magnificent four-poster bed, draped in gold and emerald-green brocade, and next to it was the most charming intricately carved wooden crib for Matilde. Dominique exclaimed her pleasure out loud when she set eyes on it. The little satin pillow and quilt inside looked hand-sewn, and were quite simply exquisite.

Sweeping her gaze round some more, she saw lush hangings made of silk on the walls, with embroidered scenes reflecting the fascinating mix of Arabic, Judaic and Christian legacies that Cristiano had informed her influenced this particular part of Spain. The antique chairs, occasional tables and clothes chests that furnished the rest of the room looked like the very finest. Her bedsit back in London resembled some Dickensian pauper's dwelling in comparison! *What must Cristiano have thought when he saw it?*

'This is just for me and Matilde?' she asked, hugging her arms over her chest in the thin petrol-blue sweater she wore with skinny black jeans. 'The pair of us could easily get lost in all this space after what we've been used to! What an amazing place you live in…I had no idea!'

'Ramón never talked about his home?' Cristiano's glance all but dissected her, it was so piercing.

Feeling a little uneasy, Dominique shrugged. 'Not really. He talked more about *you*, as a matter of fact.'

'Me?'

'He really looked up to you, you know? You were someone he admired and aspired to be like.'

Someone he'd admired and aspired to be like? Was he supposed to take heart from that, when since Ramón's death the thought had routinely niggled away at him that in the final analysis he had simply let his cousin down? *Just as he had let down his wife and child,* Cristiano reflected bitterly. He hadn't been able to save any of them. Even though he would have sacrificed everything—including his own life—so that they could live.

Frowning, he tried to push away the sense of hopelessness and futility that suddenly washed over him, but it was not easy. Finding himself staring at the slim but shapely young woman standing just a few feet away from him, with her tantalising silken rope of hair, dressed in the kind of plain and simple clothing that should not be remotely alluring at all yet somehow was, Cristiano almost swayed at the force of his desire to touch and hold her. It swept over him with all the power of something deeply primal.

Madre de Dios! What was happening to him? He was not supposed to feel this way about a girl he considered himself guardian and protector to! He knew right then that it would be extreme folly to

give in to such an impossible and dangerous urge—
that it would be like lighting the fuse to a most
lethal explosive and the fall-out would be considerable. Everything inside him felt like a coiled
spring, tightly bound, because he had to strive so
hard to control his shocking impulse…

'My family were overjoyed to see the baby…just
as I knew they would be,' he remarked, a slight
catch in his voice.

There was an urgent need to change the subject
to something lighter, to somehow tamp down this
restless, potentially perilous desire that tormented
him. It did not help his case to observe the huge
four-poster bed, positioned only inches away from
where Dominique stood.

'It is so good to see them smiling again.'

'They are incredible women! I did not realise
they…and you…had lost so many of your loved
ones. It's just so sad. If Matilde being here helps
bring happiness into the house, then I am truly glad
that I came.'

'Good.' His smile somewhat strained now,
Cristiano moved towards the door that led back into
the corridor. 'Why don't you familiarise yourself with
your new surroundings for a little while, and I will go
and arrange for your luggage to be brought up? Do
not worry about Matilde…she has three doting
women to take care of her now, and is perfectly safe.'

'Cristiano?'

'What is it?'

Suddenly she was there beside him, her peachy smell stirring the air and making his body tighten with almost shocking and violent demand as he glanced into the flawless blue mirror of her long-lashed gaze.

'Are you all right?'

'Of course. Why should I not be all right?' he answered tersely, confused that she should display such apparent concern towards him.

'It's just that I sense some tension in you. Won't you tell me what's the matter?'

She bit down on a temptingly plump lower lip that Cristiano would defy a *saint* not to want to taste and coloured deeply.

'You've been so good to me and Matilde during the past few days… If there's anything I can do to help you, you will tell me, won't you?'

To Cristiano's utter surprise, she reached out and laid her slender cool palm over his hand. Sensing what he was sure was simply meant to be comforting pressure, for a moment he was rocked to his very soul. The turmoil-inducing contact scorched along his nerve-endings like living flame.

'That is a dangerous offer, Dominique. And, trust me…it is one that you would be very wise to retract at this moment in time.'

His smile was almost bitter, as well as painfully rueful. Freeing his hand and opening the door, Cristiano stalked away from her without saying another word…

Joining them for a special homecoming meal which the women of the household—along with the housekeeper, María—had prepared for that evening was Marco, Elena's Italian boyfriend. They had recently become engaged, Elena had confided to Dominique earlier, her dark eyes glowing with excitement and pleasure. He was a slim-built and extremely handsome young man, and the couple seemed quite besotted with each other.

In fact, watching them from time to time as she hungrily tucked in to the delicious food that had been cooked in her and Matilde's honour, Dominique knew a pang of longing that wouldn't easily abate. *And it was worryingly heightened whenever she glanced Cristiano's way.* He was sitting at the head of the magnificent dining table to her left, and amid the magical glow of myriad softly flickering candles his dark eyes and sable hair glinted with the fierce sheen of polished jet.

Why had he reacted so bitterly to her offer of help earlier? His sudden unexpected coldness had hurt her. It might be wrong, and not very wise of her, but Dominique had started to see him as her friend…

someone she could trust above all. But now she indeed saw the danger of viewing such a powerful, charismatic man as him in such a way. When it came down to it he was as unpredictable and unknowable as he had been when Dominique had first met him. She was kidding herself if she dared to assume a closer bond than that.

Her stomach dived to her boots as she considered the thought that had been worrying her the most. *What if he was furious with her because he thought she'd been trying to come on to him in some way?* Reliving the scene when he'd made his terse remark, Dominique shockingly reflected on how her words might not have seemed quite innocent from Cristiano's point of view. Deeply perturbed, she reached out for the glass of ruby-red Rioja that was glimmering in the candlelight beside her plate, and almost knocked it over in her haste to lift it.

'Careful!'

Next to her, Cristiano's compelling rich voice throbbed out a warning.

Glancing up at him in alarm, Dominique grimaced. 'Sorry.'

'You do not have to apologise. You are enjoying your food?'

'It's wonderful! I'm loving it, actually… What did you say this casserole was called?'

'*Estofado de pescado*. This particular region is well known for its fish dishes.'

'Well, it's absolutely delicious!'

Across the long and magnificently laid table, Consuela caught her eye and bestowed an uninhibitedly warm smile on the younger woman. She had spent the rest of the afternoon and most of the early evening taking care of Matilde, and had even accompanied her to their bedroom to watch her settle the baby into the beautiful crib that Dominique was not surprised to learn was a family heirloom.

'Eat more!' she said, in her limited English, pushing another appetising dish in her direction. Then, turning towards her nephew, she addressed him in rapid Spanish, and it was obvious to Dominique that the conversation was about her.

'My aunt has heard that the food in England is terrible and is worried that you have been starving yourself because it is so bad!'

Cristiano grinned, and there was no strain about that sensual, rather beautiful mouth of his as he translated. Instead it was curved with genuine delight, and beneath its dazzling effect Dominique felt a little like a neglected plant that had been languishing in the shade too long and had suddenly been moved out into the sunlight.

'What?'

'She thinks that you need some more meat on

your bones, Dominique…and also that you need to be out in the sun more—because you are, in her opinion, far too pale!'

Knowing the older woman did not mean any insult, but was merely saying what she thought, Dominique sighed. 'Well, please tell Consuela that I have never starved myself in my life and never will! I certainly don't hold with all that rubbish the media push about skinny being best! And the food at home is not *that* bad! There's plenty of variety, at any rate, with all the different cultures that thrive there. As for being too pale…I'm sure the Spanish sun will soon change that—given time!'

Studying her intently for a moment, Cristiano translated what she'd said, and Consuela's concerned frown quickly turned into a pleased smile.

'*Bueno!*' She nodded and, reaching across the table, tightly squeezed Dominique's hand.

The other woman's care and attention was touching and, caught unawares, Dominique sensed the sting of tears prick the backs of her eyelids. *She had received more kindness in this household in one day than she had in years at home with her mother, and she almost didn't know how to handle it…*

'Tomorrow my aunt would like to take care of Matilde while I take you to lunch, and also show you some of the sights of our beautiful town. Does that plan meet with your approval?'

'Don't you have to get back to work?' Dominique asked Cristiano in surprise, blinking away the moisture that had helplessly surged into her eyes.

'I have made some phone calls and I do not need to be back in my office for another two days. Until then I will be here to help you settle in.'

'You don't have to do that. I'm sure you have more important things to do than play nursemaid to me and Matilde! I've already taken up too much of your time as it is.'

'What could be more important than bringing my aunt's grandchild home? And I would be very remiss in my duties indeed if I did not take proper care of you and your daughter while you are living under my roof!'

'I told you before,' Dominique retorted, dabbing her eyes with the corner of her linen napkin, suddenly feeling more vulnerable and exposed than she liked, 'I don't need anybody to take care of me!'

The truth was that something in her took great offence at the idea that Cristiano only viewed her as some kind of 'duty' he had to fulfil. His marked distance towards her since their arrival in Spain had left her longing for the return of the charming and attentive man who had walked through the park with them on a crisp winter's day, with his hand at her back, talking quietly about the many stunning vistas of Spain and the fragrant, sultry heat of his homeland that he was missing with a passion.

'Excuse me.' Politely inclining her head towards Consuela and Luisa, Dominique pushed back her chair and hurried out of the grand dining room, with its fabulous coffered ceiling and glowing candles, trying hard to get her bearings through her tears as she stood in a cavernous corridor illuminated only by the softest lamplight.

Footsteps from behind told her she had not been allowed to escape as easily as that.

'Everyone is concerned that you are not happy. What is wrong?'

Turning, she saw Cristiano walk slowly towards her, compelling and heart-stoppingly masculine, dressed in top-to-toe black, the lamplight making the carved contours of his face appear even more hauntingly arresting than usual.

'Today has been an emotional journey in more ways than one, that's all. And I'm very tired. I don't mean to offend anybody, but I'd like to go back to my room now and maybe have an early night. Will you please give your family my apologies?'

'That is not a problem. But I do not like to see you so upset.'

Before he could consider the wisdom of such a gesture, Cristiano raised his hand and touched his knuckles very gently to Dominique's tear-stained cheek. Her skin was very close to being as soft as Matilde's, and her blue eyes were so bewitching that he was in perilous danger of forgetting just why he had followed her out here in the first place.

'All I need is a good night's sleep and I'll be fine.'

'Will you, Dominique?'

His fingers slid down her cheek and under her chin. Lifting it a little, so that he had even better access to her beguiling gaze, Cristiano found himself studying her with an explosively insistent renewal of the desire he'd experienced earlier in her bedroom. His whole body was electrified by it.

'What do you—what do you mean?' Her soft voice fell to a bare whisper as she stared back at him.

Knowing he was locked in one of the fiercest battles for self-control that he'd ever experienced, still Cristiano could not help but lower his head towards the sweetly parted lips that tempted him so powerfully.

'I am not so sure a night's sleep would ease what troubles *me* right at this moment,' he said ruefully, his voice growing husky.

His mouth touched Dominique's long before he realised he had very definitely lost the battle he'd been engaged in—that in truth had been consuming him all evening…

CHAPTER SEVEN

DOMINIQUE was certain her bones were melting… As soon as Cristiano's lips had made their descent towards hers, her eyelids had closed of their own volition as she gave herself up to the sense of wonder and the most all-consuming excitement she could ever have imagined.

Divine, glorious, *essential…* These were the epithets that soared through her mind as she willingly surrendered to his kiss. Her hands held onto his lean waist, everything in her softening to welcome his opposing hardness, and she was shocked to discover what little resistance she had against this man.

The combustible contact probably only lasted just a few seconds, but in Dominique's mind it seemed to go on for ever…*perhaps because she willed it to?* In the end it was Cristiano who ended the kiss, not Dominique—even though she knew it probably should have been she who called a halt to the most devastating engagement of the senses that she'd ever had.

His dark, aroused glance reflected back to her the fact that he had been equally engaged and affected by the sensuality they had both just experienced.

'I probably should not have done that…but somehow I find that I cannot regret it. *Buenas noches,* Dominique. Sleep well.'

He turned around and strode back down the hall before Dominique even got the chance to reply, his heels hitting the ground in rhythmic staccato echoes.

Feeling even more disorientated than before, she glanced round almost dazedly at the terracotta walls with their glowing lamps, needing a moment to right herself again. She was finding it hard to believe what had just happened wasn't some astonishing dream she'd somehow conjured up because she was tired and emotional. She sighed softly and hugged herself tight…

'Tilly, Tilly! You are so silly!'

Blowing a loud raspberry on her daughter's perfectly plump little belly as the baby lay in the centre of the huge bed, arms and legs flailing in excitement and her sweet face wreathed in delighted dimples, Dominique sensed a wave of love so strong consuming her that it almost took her breath away.

Every day the bond between mother and child was growing ever more powerful, and the little girl meant the sun, moon and stars to her. Yet as she gazed lovingly down at Matilde, Dominique found herself wondering if her own mother had ever looked at *her* like that when she was so small and defenceless and had depended on her for everything. It was hard to imagine when all Dominique could recall was impatience and irritation.

Swallowing down the hurt this thought provoked, she asked herself what it was about her that was so *hard* to love. She'd always tried to do her best, to be helpful and thoughtful and not deliberately difficult. Yet even Ramón had not been able to love her…not even when he'd known she was carrying his baby. The fault surely *must* lie with her.

Her mind drifted cautiously to Cristiano's devastating kiss last night. Dominique had been trying to hold the intoxicating memory of it at bay from the moment she'd opened her eyes an hour ago and greeted the day, but now it filled her mind in glorious and vivid Technicolor, and something deep inside her ached hard with need. She was sure that in the cold light of day—despite what he had said last night—Cristiano *would* regret their passionate kiss. And now Dominique had to shore up her defences even more firmly against the growing attraction she felt towards him, and learn to keep her distance whenever she could. *She'd been hurt enough.* She did not want to be hurt so badly ever again…

'Come on, Tilly! There's a good girl. Let's put this lovely new dress on you, shall we? Your grandmother is looking after you this afternoon, and I think you should look your best for her, don't you?'

The knock on her sitting room door startled her. Glancing down at her pyjama-clad figure, Dominique reached for the robe at the end of the magnificent bed and quickly put it on. Thinking it might be her daughter's doting new grandmother, come to wish her grandchild good morning, she scooped the half-dressed baby up in her arms and hurried out to see if she was right.

But it was not Consuela Cordova who was waiting. It was her ebony-eyed, broad-shouldered and handsome nephew, dressed in crisp white shirt and jeans and looking unexpectedly and disturbingly more relaxed than Dominique had ever seen him.

'Buenos días!' He smiled, and his teeth were very white against his beautiful bronzed skin.

'Good morning,' she answered, a distinct husky catch in her voice.

'My mother and my aunt have already breakfasted, but I have been waiting for you and Matilde,' he explained.

Then, before Dominique could respond, he reached out his arms for the baby, who was busily chewing on her soggy drool-covered thumb as her mother held her.

Her daughter was completely at ease and smiling as she handed her over. Was there *any* female who wouldn't be similarly delighted to find Cristiano Cordova on her doorstep? Dominique wondered, a rogue shiver of pleasure rippling through her.

'*Buenos días* to you too, my beautiful little angel! Did you sleep well? Did you? We must have a little chat about all the sweet dreams you must have had!'

'You shouldn't have waited for us,' Dominique told him, flustered, as he swept past her into the room, murmuring baby talk to a clearly entranced Matilde.

'I wanted to.' Glancing away from the baby for a moment, fixing his attention on Dominique instead, he shrugged and then smiled again. 'Now, go and get yourself ready and I will wait here with Matilde.'

'I need to finish putting on her dress.'

'Give it to me and I will do it.'

His tone clearly brooked no argument, and with her legs stupidly trembling Dominique went and fetched the dress and brought it back to him.

'Now go! We will be perfectly all right here until you return—won't we, Matilde?'

There was something utterly sexy and compelling about a man who could be relied upon to take care of a baby, Dominique thought as she hurriedly showered and dressed. Then, guiltily catching herself, she remembered her vow not to get too emotionally attached to Cristiano unless she wanted to invite a whole mountain of trouble to come crashing down on her!

'Concentrate!' she exclaimed out loud.

Pushing her fingers irritably through her newly washed and dried hair, she quickly plaited it, then nervously surveyed the very spartan selection of clothing she'd brought that now hung in the huge antique wardrobe. Cristiano had said something about taking her to lunch. Dominique hoped it would be somewhere fairly casual rather than upmarket, because she didn't even *possess* an item of clothing that was what you could call dressy.

It occurred to her that she might be expected to wear something sombre, in deference to Ramón's death. The idea was too depressing to be contemplated—and surely Cristiano would have mentioned it if that were the case?

Telling herself not to get too hung up about clothes, she picked out a fairly demure knee-length dress with a colourful floral design and a band of blue ribbon that went around the ribcage, underneath her breasts. If the day were as warm as yesterday, then it would surely fit the bill? She could already feel the heat through the opened patio doors, and she paused to savour its sultry kiss as the evocative perfume of the new morning filled her senses. The house was on a hillside, not too far from a mountain range, and consequently the air was quite intoxicating.

'I'm ready. Sorry if I kept you waiting.'

Cristiano's heart slammed hard against his ribcage as Dominique walked back into the sitting room. He already knew she had a good figure, but in the pretty summer dress she was wearing he discovered it was actually quite sensational. Her legs were long and shapely, and thankfully not too thin. She had slender, elegant calves, and a tiny waist, and Cristiano realised that her shape was definitely more hourglass than straight up and down. Her dress showcased her attributes perfectly, and the scooped neckline of the bodice allowed a glimpse of cleavage that was simply...*arresting*.

Suddenly becoming aware that he had still not said anything but was just staring—like a schoolboy with a crush on his teacher—he pushed to his feet from the couch with Matilde in his arms, briefly inclining his head.

'Very nice. That is a very charming dress you are wearing, Dominique. It will not do a lot to help my blood pressure today, but still...I definitely appreciate it.'

He knew the look he gave Dominique to accompany his words was provocative, but Cristiano could not help himself. Waking up this morning with the memory of those sweet lips of hers pliant, warm and sexy beneath his, and now seeing her in that sultry little dress was doing nothing less than adding fuel to the fire that was already simmering inside him…

'If you think it's not suitable then I'll change into something else.'

'I did not say it was not suitable, and I do not want you to change. You have a beautiful figure, Dominique… You are young and lovely, and I do not expect you to dress like a nun!'

'Your mother and your aunt won't think I'm—' Frowning, she still seemed unconvinced about the dress. 'They won't think I'm being disrespectful? Wearing something so colourful, I mean?'

'Because Consuela is wearing the garb of mourning?' Slowly Cristiano shook his head. 'No. In years gone by it was customary for the widow or the mother of a man who had died to wear black for quite some time—even the rest of her life if she chose— but now it is up to the woman concerned, and clearly it does not apply to you, Dominique. Please…just relax. And now we should go down to breakfast. I am sure this little one is as hungry as I am!'

'She's had her bottle this morning, but I've also brought some baby cereal from home for her. I'll just go and get it.'

* * *

'I may have to hold your hand so that I do not lose you. It is very busy today because Christmas is so near.'

Before they went to lunch, Cristiano had decided to take Dominique to the gypsy market. The colourful stallholders sold their wares all over Spain, but in his opinion the market that was held in their own historic little town was one of the best. Smiling at Dominique as people bustled around them, eagerly examining the goods on sale—from clothing to jewellery, ceramics to shoes—he saw that his companion was completely transfixed by it all. *And holding her hand was not exactly something he found difficult,* Cristiano thought ironically.

Every time he glanced her way, and her clear blue eyes met his, he had to practically fight off the almost overpowering need to touch her. Not wanting to delve into the reason for this impulse too closely, he decided to simply enjoy the day and take the opportunity of seeing the places that were so familiar to him through Dominique's captivated eyes.

'I'll be all right,' she answered him, her gaze almost deliberately avoiding his. 'I'll make sure I stay close. Oh, look! They're selling Christmas trees!'

Gravitating to a large area where the most traditional Christmas decoration of all was displayed, in almost unbelievable abundance, Dominique stared wistfully at the trees for sale.

'Will *you* have a Christmas tree?' she asked.

'Of course. In fact I know that we have one being delivered to the house the day after tomorrow. Elena and my aunt usually decorate it together. They will also be putting out the *belén*—remember I told you about that?'

'The nativity scene? Yes…I remember.'

'And tomorrow night the Christmas lights will be turned on in all the towns and cities across the country. There will also be parades and processions, and the churches will be filled with people.'

'Do you think your family might let me join in when they decorate the tree?'

Dominique gazed at Cristiano with all the heart-felt yearning of a child long denied such a magical privilege, and he thought about the cold comfort her mother offered at Christmas and was disturbed by how angry he felt.

'We will all do it together,' he promised, his glance settling intently on her face and this time not allowing her to easily avoid it. 'Even Matilde must be included. I know my aunt will insist on it!'

'She seems to really love Tilly already.'

'She has loved her since the moment she learned of her existence! Her grandchild being here has made the world of difference to her. Instead of dreading the future, she now wants to live to a very old age so that she can see Matilde grow up to be a woman with a family of her own!'

'Thank you.'

'For what?' Cristiano's dark brows drew together in puzzlement.

'For bringing me to Spain and letting me be a part of all this…' Gesturing at the busy, colourful market around her, Dominique smiled, shy and tentative.

'You are most welcome.' He bowed his head towards her in a formal manner almost from a bygone age, and was silently delighted when her eyes widened to the size of dinner plates in response.

From time to time—inevitably, perhaps—Cristiano spied a face that he knew in the crowd, and immediately engaged in conversation. Inevitably too a curious gaze would go to Dominique, and he would have to introduce her.

Seeing how it made her uncomfortable to receive their condolences about Ramón, he made the decision to cut short their visit and leave for the hilltop restaurant where they were lunching instead. But as they prepared to leave the bustling market behind he spied the most exquisite sapphire-blue shawl on a stall displaying many beautiful silks and scarves—it was almost the same vivid hue as Dominique's eyes.

Steering the surprised young woman beside him towards it, he nodded at the plump grey-haired holder whose stall it was, and whose own generous shoulders were covered in a bright scarlet version. Gesturing towards the blue silk, Cristiano asked her how much it was and then bartered her down to a lesser, more reasonable figure, as was the custom. When the item had been wrapped and paid for, he drew Dominique to one side and gave it to her.

'It matches your eyes,' he told her, his voice lowering. 'And it will be perfect to wear later on, when the sun goes down and the evening gets cooler.'

As she accepted the gift he placed into her hands, he was touched to see her lips tremble ever so slightly as she received it.

'It's—it's too kind of you, and it's absolutely beautiful! Thank you, Cristiano.'

The way she said his name, in her reserved English accent, made his insides flood with warmth. He liked it. The trouble was he thought perhaps he liked it a little *too* much, and that immediately alerted him to the fact that he was not keeping his guard up against her charms as strictly as he should be.

Grimly, Cristiano made himself remember what had happened to Martina and their baby, and as ice flowed into his blood instead of heat he found his ardour for the pretty young woman beside him thankfully ebb…

CHAPTER EIGHT

AT THE restaurant they sat outside, like many other diners, enjoying the warmth of the sun and the stunning views of the mountains in the distance. Viewed from a stranger's perspective, Dominique was sure she blended in perfectly with everybody else…a tourist, perhaps, having a relaxing lunch with a handsome friend, husband…or *lover*… She flinched at that last too disturbing possibility. Yes, outside she might appear to be calm and at ease, but inside…inside she was in utter turmoil.

The gift of the stunning sapphire shawl from Cristiano had all but undone her. So had the comment he had made about her eyes. Coupled with his deeply stirring kiss last night, she barely knew what to do with the wildly impossible thoughts she was having.

'You are not eating.'

Glancing up, she tumbled headlong into the compelling velvet darkness of Cristiano's searching gaze. 'I'm just trying to take it all in…the beautiful day… that breathtaking view of the mountains…the fact that I'm here in Spain and Matilde has been reunited with a grandmother who loves her. I might have to pinch myself to check that I'm not dreaming!'

'So…you are happy?' A corner of his beautiful mouth quirked upwards into his smooth-shaven cheek. 'Happier at least than when you were in England on your own?'

'I won't pretend it wasn't tough. Being a single mother is hard enough, but to be honest I think there's a conspiracy of silence about raising children amongst those who have them! Because it's viewed as such an everyday event it's assumed it should be somehow easy, when actually it's probably one of the hardest things a human being could ever do!'

'But you do not regret having Matilde?'

'Never! How could I? She's the most wonderful thing that's ever happened to me! I'd die if anything happened to her!'

'Well…' Raising his wine glass to his lips, Cristiano's tanned brow creased thoughtfully. 'One day you will meet a good man, get married, and she will have the father she deserves.'

Why did his comment not cheer her in the way he obviously meant it to? Dominique reflected dolefully. Of course she didn't want to spend the rest of her life raising her daughter on her own, but after Ramón's desertion thinking about meeting someone else was the furthest thing from her mind. Yet when she was with Cristiano she sensed herself becoming more and more entranced by him. And seeing the way he was with his family—so caring and protective—and how he was so natural with a small infant like Matilde, didn't help her vow to keep her distance for fear of future hurt—but something told her it was already too late for that anyway...

'That will not be for a long time yet, I'm sure.' Laying her fork down beside her plate, she touched her napkin to her lips, inexplicably feeling her heart race.

'You are not the kind of woman who should be alone, Dominique.'

'What makes you say that? I've been managing all these years on my own, more or less!'

'But that does not mean you have to continue managing on your own.'

'Let's change the subject, shall we?' It was hard not to react defensively when Cristiano was touching upon the one issue that never made her feel very good. 'Relationships are unfortunately my Achilles' Heel, and that's just the way it is! No matter how hard I try, I'm just no good at them!'

'Be careful that doesn't become a self-fulfilling

prophecy,' Cristiano warned darkly, his expression without humour.

Why did Dominique get the curious feeling he was not just talking about her? What was his story? she mused silently. Why wasn't an amazing man like him married, with at least half a dozen kids to dote on? He was clearly devoted to family, and appeared to genuinely love children. *Yet there was something behind those fascinating eyes of his that Dominique had glimpsed once or twice that bothered her...something that suggested he had been badly wounded by someone too...*

'This is really very good,' she said, digging her fork into the fragrant rice dish in front of her, knowing she was deliberately trying to deflect further discussion about a topic that caused her more grief than any other. 'Though it's hard to concentrate on food with the fantastic view.'

'Yes,' Cristiano agreed, his steady gaze lingering long on Dominique's face. 'The view is...rather compelling...'

Later that evening Dominique found herself in the library. She had mentioned to Luisa that she had forgotten to bring a book to read, and the older woman had kindly brought her to this magnificent repository of books of all kinds—many, as she had proudly told Dominique, in English. Her husband had been a great reader, and so was Cristiano, and he often brought books back with him from his travels. After Luisa had left her to go and help prepare the evening meal, and while Matilde was under the protective wing of her grandmother in the sitting room, it was really pleasant for Dominique to have some time in which to relax on her own for a little while.

As she scanned the generously filled bookshelves, she was inadvertently distracted by a group of photographs that hung on the wall. Her interest piqued, she found herself gravitating there to inspect them more closely. But before she could do so the library door opened behind her, and the man she seemed to spend an ever-increasing amount of time trying not to think about entered the room. He was dressed casually but smartly, in another elegant white shirt teamed with black trousers tailored to perfection, and his dark hair looked glossily damp in the light that shone from the hall behind him. Dominique realised he must have recently showered for dinner.

Without saying anything, he shut the door behind him and slowly came into the room to join her. She sucked in a breath. When he was just inches away from her, he spoke. 'My mother told me I would find you in here. I do not mean to intrude upon your privacy, but I thought you might like some help navigating what we have. Tell me what kind of books you like and I will point you in the right direction.'

'Oh…I like all kinds of books. Biographies, novels, history… Do you have anything about the region where you live?'

Dominique's tongue briefly stole out to wet her suddenly dry lips. *Cristiano was standing way too close… She could barely remember her own name, let alone expound on what kind of books she liked reading when he stood so near!*

'*Sí.*' He shrugged those wide shoulders of his as though her answer amused him. 'Of course. We have *many* books on that subject. We have a fascinating history, as I am sure you can tell just by glancing at the architecture around you. But you surprise me, Dominique. I would have thought you were more in the mood for a novel of some kind. *A Christmas Carol,* perhaps, bearing in mind the season we are in?'

'Dickens is a wonderful writer, but honestly I don't think I have the concentration for a novel right now. My mind is all over the place!'

'Oh?' His gaze was seemingly transfixed on her lips, and Dominique froze. 'Why is that?'

'Wh-why?'

'I see that you are wearing the shawl I bought you,' he commented.

Disturbingly, he moved closer. So close that she

could see every minute detail of his arrestingly attractive face in sharp focus—from the coal-black sweep of his long lashes to the darker shadow of beard grazing his hard, lean jaw, with that Cordova dimple in the chin that Matilde had so charmingly inherited. She was startlingly aware too of the exotic tang of his aftershave which, combined with the seductive male heat he emanated, was putting her senses under extreme intoxicating duress. Dominique had no will to tear her gaze away for even a second.

'I was right. It perfectly matches the colour of your eyes.'

'It does? Well, I—'

She was stunned into silence when Cristiano placed his hands either side of her face, his hypnotic gaze holding hers with heart-pounding purpose, and Dominique knew what he intended long before the explosive touch of his lips on hers obliterated every coherent thought in her head.

This time it was no exploratory kiss—executed, perhaps, with the aim of helping her forget her worries for a while and relax… No. This was the full-blown, hungry kiss of a man caught in the grip of inflamed desire, and Dominique had never in her life been the recipient of such raw, passionate need.

His tongue thrust into her mouth with almost brutal command, and a heat started to burn inside her that made her shake and fear for her very sanity. Her hands reached out to steady herself against Cristiano, her fingers biting into the iron-hard flesh of his waist as her own escalating need suddenly outran any whispered caution in her head to stop this now and be sensible. It was simply heavenly to be wanted and desired this much, and Dominique started to kiss Cristiano back just as feverishly and wantonly as he was kissing her, her heart open wide and her senses more intensely alive than they'd ever been before.

Ramón had kissed her with the clumsily selfish needs of an over-eager boy, but Cristiano was without doubt kissing her like a *man*. And when his hand cupped her breast and he moved his thumb devastatingly back and forth across the rigid velvet tip beneath her thin summer dress, Dominique's hips felt as if they had melted right down to the bone. Her mouth slid away from his with a soft groan of pleasure as he ground his tight, lean hips against hers, the tender flesh of her cheekbone grazing against the harshness of his studded jaw. Impinging on her besieged senses was the shocking primal evidence of Cristiano's need, and Dominique's legs seemed to turn to liquid rubber that could not possibly sustain her upright position for long.

'I will lock the door,' Cristiano whispered against

her ear, brushing his mouth briefly but devastatingly across her tender lobe.

Before she could absorb the earth-shattering meaning of such a statement he left her to do just that. With the touch of a button he dimmed the lights too, and Dominique stared at him as he returned, wondering how a man as beautiful and perfect as he could possibly want an unconfident and ordinary girl like her, when he could probably have any stunning woman he wanted.

'Everyone is busy and will not miss us for a while,' he told her, and before she had an inkling of what he intended Cristiano slid his arm around her waist and lifted her bodily up into his arms.

Her heart was racing so fast inside her chest that Dominique seriously feared for her ability to remain conscious. Finding herself gently lowered onto a sumptuous red velvet chaise-longue that was positioned by the unlit fireplace, she stared wide-eyed and nervous up into the riveting handsome face that gazed down at her.

'I want to make love to you…I have been thinking about it all day,' he told her. 'In fact…the idea has been *consuming* me.'

Dominique reacted purely on instinct. Reaching up, she urged his face down towards hers. The time between kisses had been far too long, in her opinion, and she was unashamedly hungry for the taste of his lips again. He had a taste like no other man she'd ever known, and it was both intoxicating and addictive.

Her delightful blue shawl slid away from her shoulders, its delicate fringe brushing against the exposed flesh of her slender arms revealed by her dress. She heard the thud of Cristiano's shoes as they hit the floor, and a little throb of shock pulsed through her. Just before he touched his achingly seductive mouth to hers Dominique sensed the pleasure she'd been longing for about to sweep her away—as easily as some flimsy raft on a compelling sea. 'Please don't regret this...' she said softly. 'That's all I ask.'

For a moment his avid glance stole her soul. *'Nunca...* Never!'

His seductive reply was as fervent as Dominique had hoped it would be. Arms entwined around him, she felt Cristiano's muscular weight press her down deep into the velvet fabric of the couch beneath her. The hard, masculine warmth of his body seemed to seep into her marrow, making everything inside her tense so hard with need that she felt she might snap in two.

Shifting his position slightly, he started to touch her intimately with his hands and his mouth...exploring, kneading, tasting...and Dominique could not contain the uncontrollable tremors that were the result of his devastating sensual attention.

'You are so soft…so incredibly beautiful,' he whispered against her ear as his hands—which had been moving back and forth across her pelvis—finally moved lower, dragging up the hem of her dress and, with destroying purpose, cupping her through the flimsy cotton of her panties.

Even as Dominique felt her breath catch, Cristiano inserted his finger into the heat and moisture that drenched her there. Pushing her dress up further, he let his hot mouth fall upon her aching breasts contained by the simple white cotton bra, his lips and tongue giving them equal attention as his fingers worked their irresistible magic between her thighs. Dominique felt herself drowning in the erotic pleasure that consumed her like hot, licking flame ripping through a tinder-dry forest.

A harsh gasp left her throat and, captured by the sound, Cristiano diverted his attention from her breasts to her mouth, claiming it passionately as his fingers moved rhythmically faster and deeper inside her.

Learning intimately what the expression 'seeing stars' meant, Dominique bit down hard on her lip to try and contain her cry as she climaxed, shutting her eyes against a pleasure so wild and yet so profound that she couldn't help but release tears.

'Dominique? Look at me.'

Her eyes flew open again at the huskily voiced

request, and her already fast-beating heart galloped even more when she saw the expression of primal need and hunger etched into the striking contours of Cristiano's bronzed face.

'What is it?'

'You are crying… Is it because I caused you pain?'

His concern was such that Dominique's heart stalled. She hurried to reassure him.

'No. No—of course not! I just…' Hesitating over what she had been going to say—because she did not want to refer to Ramón and the intimacy she had shared with him, which had been nowhere *near* as satisfying—Dominique tried to explain her feelings another way. 'I was crying because what you— what you did gave me such pleasure, Cristiano! It made me feel a little emotional…that's all.'

'Do you know how much *more* pleasure I want to give you? I am almost in physical pain with the desire to be inside you!' Cristiano's voice was rough with need as he slid his hand behind Dominique's head and angled it towards him, his voracious glance devouring every inch of her startled face. 'But I realise this is not the place for me to join with you as I long to! Tonight…after everyone has retired and Matilde is fast asleep…I will come to you. Leave your door unlocked…*sí*?'

Should she come to her senses and say no? All Dominique knew was that she ached down to her very soul to have him possess her in the way he so candidly described, and to refuse him would be like denying herself vital oxygen to breathe. She wasn't about to do any such thing.

'All right,' she whispered, tenderly cupping his face.

He kissed her passionately then, as if to brand her with his taste and leave her with the tantalising promise of what lay ahead in the night to come…

CHAPTER NINE

THROUGHOUT the delicious meal that had been placed before him Cristiano merely toyed with the food on his plate. It was as if some strange exotic disease afflicted him, making him feel light-headed almost to the point of dizziness. His heart raced and his stomach clenched as if it was trapped in a vice. *And the symptoms were heightened whenever his gaze happened to alight on Dominique.*

Dominique…the bewitching young woman that his irresponsible cousin had got pregnant and abandoned without even the most basic financial assistance with which to raise his child. The woman Cristiano had sworn to protect and watch over until such time as some other man…her future husband… took on the responsibility. The woman he now lusted after as he had lusted after no other woman before… Even his *wife*, God rest her soul.

He could hardly believe what was happening to

him. Before he had pledged himself to Martina, Cristiano had enjoyed seducing women just as much as any other red-blooded male. But his need to be near Dominique—to know where she was when she wasn't in his sight, to hear her voice, to gaze at her and wonder what it would feel like to have that long unbound hair of hers trickle freely through his fingers, to have her unique scent saturate his senses—it was like some unstoppable force of nature that he scarce had any control over.

For the past two years he had steered clear of romantic entanglements like a driver taking an immediate detour whenever a potential traffic jam loomed on the horizon. Nothing could have prepared him for the powerful feelings running through his body and mind whenever he even *thought* about Dominique—let alone spent time with her. And this afternoon, when he had deliberately sought her out in the library, locked the door and engaged her in the most *intimate* way… Cristiano almost had to suppress a groan as he recalled the experience.

As though sensing his passionate discomfort, Dominique glanced across the table at him just then, and he saw the surge of colour that tinted her cheeks to a most delightful rose-pink. Dry-mouthed, he let his glance fall to the scooped neckline of the dress she was wearing, and the enticing shadow of cleavage it revealed. She had the most lush, perfect breasts…*breasts that Cristiano's mouth had become acquainted with only a few short hours ago.*

When he thought of the night that lay ahead he tried to quash any qualms that arose in his mind about the wisdom—or lack of it—of what he was anticipating by fiercely asserting that he would not be reckless. He would absolutely protect Dominique against another situation like the one that had manifested itself with Ramón. And he reassured himself that their being together the way he yearned for could not be wrong when she had made it so clear to him that it was what she desired too…

Dominique had lain in the bathtub for ages after Matilde had gone to sleep. She had scattered a handful of fragrant rose petals in the steamy hot water—a gift that had been left in a beautifully presented jar, along with many other expensive toiletries on the marble surround for her exclusive use. Lounging back in the gently lapping perfumed water, she felt as close to the legendary Cleopatra as a girl could get. She might not be bathing in asses' milk but this luxurious alternative was seriously hard to beat!

As soon as she started to relax, one subject asserted itself in Dominique's mind above all the rest. *Cristiano and his promised visit.* Even though the air was filled with steam, she sensed a shiver of delicious anticipation quiver through her. Their encounter this afternoon in the library had been beyond words, but it had left her hungry for more of his thrilling touch.

Her excitement was only dampened by one question… *Was she the biggest fool that ever lived where men were concerned?* Why didn't it seem to be an even halfway viable option to resist Cristiano's devastating attraction? *It was a dangerous game she was playing.* And she was the one who was going to get hurt—not him.

Her disquiet increased. He had already mentioned that he expected that she would meet someone else one day and get married. Surely the subtext of that assertion was that she would then be off his hands, leaving him free to enjoy the bachelor status Dominique guessed he guarded so jealously? And why wouldn't he, when he was rich, gorgeous and successful? Who could blame him if he wanted to play the field instead of settling down? All that was probably on the cards with him for Dominique was a brief, intense affair.

A frustrated sigh escaped her. *If only Cristiano hadn't been so persistent in trying to help her!* If only he hadn't acted so honourably on his cousin's behalf and brought her back to Spain, united her daughter with her grandmother and given Dominique the opportunity for a far better life than she'd ever known before! All these amazing things had worked their magic on her sensitive heartstrings more than anything else—even more than the sizzling attraction that now flared between them. And now her situation was as precarious as a novice trapeze artist balancing on a high wire…

By the time she'd vacated the sensually fragrant bath serious doubt had set in about the whole affair. And once she'd dried herself off, put on a short cotton nightdress and climbed into bed, Dominique told herself that when Cristiano showed up she would tell him she'd changed her mind about them being intimate. That she'd decided it was best if they just stayed friends rather than risk spoiling everything if they became lovers…

But midnight came and went, and there was no sign of the man whose visit she'd anticipated with such nervous excitement and trepidation. Hurt that he'd obviously come to the conclusion himself that their nocturnal assignation wasn't a good idea, Dominique switched off her bedside lamp and lay back in the darkness, feeling slightly ill. *Why hadn't he come?* Had he recognised somehow that she was too needy and been put off? God knew she had tried so hard to contain her emotions and feelings around him, tried to let him see only that her intention was to be independent and not depend upon *any* man again!

But then she had been so eager when he had kissed her, touched her. She had hardly pushed him away!

Oh, God...why couldn't she ever get it right? Turning her face dejectedly into the pillow, Dominique reluctantly closed her eyes. As profound disappointment and an inevitable sense of rejection washed over her, she prayed she would soon escape her distress in the dreamy avenues of sleep...

'*Buenos diás,* Dominique.'

Everything in her tightened at the sound of that arresting rich voice, but she did not glance round. In the large but homely kitchen, giving her daughter her breakfast, Dominique was halfway to Matilde's mouth with a spoonful of oatmeal when Cristiano finally put in an appearance. The other members of his family had long since eaten and gone out again, leaving her with some precious time to spend alone with Matilde. She wondered that Cristiano had the *nerve* to wish her good morning after so casually standing her up last night, but told herself that whatever happened she mustn't let him see how upset she was.

'Morning.' Dominique murmured the word beneath her breath, and was startled when Cristiano dropped down onto the bench opposite her at the long pine table, ruefully tunnelling his fingers through his midnight-black hair. There were dark smudges beneath his eyes, as if he had hardly slept, but she steeled herself against feeling the slightest bit of sympathy for him.

'I am sorry about last night,' he ground out, the huskiness in his voice making her spine tingle.

'Are you?' Scooping another spoonful of cereal from the cheerful yellow bowl in front of her, Dominique briskly popped it into Matilde's eagerly waiting mouth. 'I'm not. With hindsight I can see that it would have been the very *worst* of mistakes, and you not showing up has thankfully helped me come to my senses!'

'Please do not say that!'

When Cristiano would have reached for her hand, Dominique deliberately moved it out of his way.

'I *wanted* to come to you…more than you can even imagine!' he insisted. 'But I asked myself if I was being entirely fair to *you*, Dominique. You have already had cause to doubt the integrity of one Cordova…I did not want to put you in a similar position again. I did not want you to think that I was taking advantage of you simply because you are staying in my house and we have developed an attraction for one another.'

'Well…whatever your reasons, you did me a big favour, Cristiano! I'm obviously too damn trusting for my own good! This latest incident has only confirmed that. There's no need for you to give it another second's thought. Let's just put it behind us and carry on as normal until I leave to go back to England—okay?'

'*Como?* Since when did you decide that you *were* going back to England?'

Even as he asked the question, everything in Cristiano clamoured silently in violent protest. *Fear of risking his heart and his soul had kept him out of Dominique's bed last night, and this was the price he was to pay for it! Dios mío!* He had wrestled with the twin demons of fear and desire *all* night, and now he realised his decision not to go to her was going to drive her away. He could see by the hurt and confusion on her lovely face that she had taken his non-appearance as nothing less than pure rejection, and he could hardly blame her.

'Since I woke up this morning! Anyway…I told you I wasn't sure if I would stay on after Christmas. It doesn't mean I won't keep in touch with Consuela and the rest of the family. I'll come back for visits whenever I can.'

'No! That is not good enough!'

His fist came down on the table and rattled the crockery. Matilde's lips trembled and she stared at Cristiano in obvious trepidation. Seeing her sweet little face very close to tears, Cristiano was immediately contrite—though no less angry with Dominique for her disagreeable announcement.

'I am sorry, *mi ángel*…I did not mean to frighten you,' he murmured to the baby and, leaning towards her, tenderly stroked her cheek. Lifting his gaze to Dominique, he ruefully shook his head. 'Do not punish my family because you are mad at me,' he said gruffly. 'They want you to stay…*I* want you to stay!'

'Matilde needs a wash. Excuse me.'

Getting to her feet with the baby in her arms, Dominique barely glanced at Cristiano. Again he silently cursed himself for making her distance herself from him like this when secretly he craved anything *but* distance between them!

'Come back and have a cup of coffee with me?' he suggested lightly.

He could see by the look in her blue eyes that she was torn for a moment, and Cristiano felt hope flare in his heart. But then she wrenched her glance free and walked to the door.

'I have some Christmas cards to write,' she murmured. 'I'll see you later.'

Back in the library after dinner, still brooding over what had happened the previous night, and still hurt that Cristiano had not sought her out for a private conversation for the rest of the day since their encounter at breakfast, Dominique found herself once again drawn to the group of photographs she had been going to examine yesterday.

One large colour portrait dominated all the rest. It consisted of three men in a formal family pose. In the centre was an older man, with thick greying hair and rather kind dark eyes, and on either side of him stood Ramón and Cristiano. The picture must have been taken a good seven or eight years ago at least, Dominique reflected, because Ramón looked not much more than a boy. Her heart squeezed as a shaft of pain went through it. *It was hard to believe he was dead.*

But, despite her sorrow at a young life taken too soon, it was Cristiano's image that drew her gaze the most. It was almost a shock to see him apparently so relaxed and happy—happier than Dominique had ever seen him. And what caught her eye too was the glint of gold on what would be his wedding finger. Her stomach executed a dizzying somersault. What had happened to his wife? Why was she never mentioned by anyone? Were they divorced? Had she had left Cristiano for another man? Such a scenario seemed hardly conceivable!

Behind her the door creaked open, and with a frisson of surprise she saw the man she'd been contemplating in the photograph standing there in the flesh.

'I have been looking for you,' he told her.

'Have you?' Wary of letting her guard down

around him again, Dominique shrugged. 'And I thought you'd been avoiding me for most of the day!'

'Then you thought wrong.' He sighed. 'That was taken about seven years ago,' he commented as he walked towards her, his glance leaving her to settle on the photograph she'd been studying. 'The man in the centre is my father, José. I suppose you have been looking at Ramón?'

Drawing the vivid blue shawl that Cristiano had bought her at the gypsy market more securely about her shoulders, Dominique glanced up at him, and she was certain her heart missed a beat. The pain in his voice as he'd asked the question was palpable, and her sudden need to help ease it in some way was intense.

'Actually…I was looking at *you*,' she confessed, her blue eyes directly meeting his.

'Oh?'

'You look—you look so content… And I noticed that you're wearing a wedding ring?'

Before she'd spoken Cristiano had appeared as though he was going to smile at her, but the instant Dominique mentioned the wedding ring his face changed completely. The deeply contoured slashes that denoted his cheekbones were sucked in sharply, and the broad banks of his wide shoulders seemed to visibly tense in what appeared to Dominique to be a potentially explosive cocktail of pain and anger.

'That was another life. One that I do not particularly want to discuss in casual conversation!'

Stung, Dominique retaliated. 'Just because I
mentioned the fact you were wearing a wedding
ring doesn't mean that I treat the idea of your
marriage remotely "casually", Cristiano! Anything
but! Something told me when we first met that you
had been badly hurt by someone. Until last night I
thought that we—that we were becoming *close…*
that you might trust me enough to confide in me.
Don't you think it's absolutely normal that I might
be interested in your past? It's not my intention to
hurt you by bringing it up!'

'You do not have to intend hurt… Talking about
that particular phase in my life inevitably *does*
inflict pain, Dominique!'

Sensing the debilitating tightening in the area of
his chest that always responded thus at the memory
of his wife and baby, Cristiano fought to get past the
waves of grief so that what he said would make
some sense. Strangely, he suddenly realised that he
did not feel as vehemently opposed to discussing
what had happened as he usually did. *Was that
because he did indeed feel that he could trust
Dominique with knowledge of the most tragic event
of his life and knew she would not abuse that trust?*

He had come in search of her because he could
barely stand another second of being without her

company, and he'd wanted the opportunity to try in some way to heal the rift that had come between them since this morning. Cristiano did not want to give the appearance of rejecting her again by refusing to be drawn about his past.

'Martina and I were married for three years. Just over two years ago she died, giving birth to our baby. Our child did not survive. The surgeons could not save either of them.' He had automatically crossed his arms over his chest, as if subconsciously protecting his heart, and he sensed Dominique's little sigh of shock feather softly over him. Cristiano grimaced. 'She knew she was taking a huge risk in becoming pregnant, given her history—but she kept the knowledge from me until it was too late.'

'Cristiano—I'm so sorry!'

Her lovely blue eyes were glassy with tears, and instead of dwelling on his own tragedy, Cristiano found himself wondering how *anyone* could thoughtlessly cause this incredible woman pain when she clearly had a heart wider than any ocean on the map?

Suddenly the need to have her in his arms became overwhelming, and he closed the gap between them in one stride, drawing her urgently against his chest. Before Dominique could utter a word Cristiano desperately sought her mouth, claiming a hard, hot kiss that he honestly wished could go on for ever. But at some point he did come up for air, and when he glanced down into Dominique's flushed, beautiful face, he registered the piercing need her features revealed with a bone-deep ache unlike any he had ever known before...

'Tonight,' he murmured, unable to deny her need any longer. 'Will you allow me to come to you?'

Equally unable to deny him, despite the heart-break of the night before, Dominique nodded her acceptance...

Her heart seemed to be breaking with sadness. She was dreaming of snow and Christmas trees, and her mother not loving her, and a tear slid from beneath her lashes and dampened her cheek. Something gentle brushed it away and a soft sigh escaped her.

The wonderful sensation of warm hands cupping her face made Dominique suddenly turn rigid as she realised this was no dream, and her eyelids flew open in shock. In the moonlight that filtered into the room through the partially opened drapes, Cristiano's dark eyes gleamed back at her, and his sensual lips curved into a smile that was as seductive as it was concerned.

'You were crying.' His rich velvet voice was pitched deliberately low in deference to the baby sleeping peacefully in her crib.

'A bad dream...' Husky with sleep, Dominique's

reply was barely above a whisper, but to her own hypersensitive hearing her heart beat loud enough to awaken the whole household.

'Will you let me help chase the bad dream away?'

'I thought you'd changed your mind again…that you weren't going to come…'

'I am sorry about that, *mi ángel*.' His rueful sigh feathered over her. 'Consuela knocked on my door and wanted to talk. She is overwhelmed by the knowledge that her grandchild is here with her at last, and was feeling somewhat emotional. Naturally she wanted to discuss Ramón too. I did not want to hurry her away.'

'Of course not!'

'But at the same time I could barely contain my frustration at not being with you! I want you so much!'

Thrilled to hear him say it, Dominique was about to tell Cristiano she felt the same—but found her declaration shockingly silenced by the hungry press of his warm, tantalising lips against hers. At the first inflammable touch of that erotic satin mouth heat poured through her body like liquid fire. Actual tremors rippled through her.

It was as she feverishly pushed the satin quilt aside to let Cristiano join her that Dominique realised he was naked to the waist and that the only clothing he wore was a pair of silk mulberry-coloured boxer shorts. As far as male bodies went, his definitely had the 'wow' factor—in spades. She saw for herself the strongly delineated collarbone and the wide, powerful shoulders above a hard-muscled bronzed torso and stomach where not a single ounce of spare flesh found a home. No wonder his clothes looked so good on him!

Helplessly transfixed, Dominique noticed too the erotic coating of silky dark hair dusting his nipples, and as her feverish gaze dared lower, past taut, lean hips, she saw the way another fine smattering led a provocative trail into the waistband of his boxers.

But there was little time for her appreciative perusal of his mouthwatering masculinity when, with a harsh groan of need, Cristiano suddenly took command of her mouth like a man presented with his first proper meal after being released from solitary confinement. He devoured her as if he would never get enough, and *never* be satisfied... And with his ravishing velvet tongue he introduced Dominique to a wild eroticism she hadn't even known existed until then. There wasn't a corner or crevice of her mouth that he didn't plunder with destroying command and brand with his addictive masculine flavours.

Lying beneath Cristiano's hard, lean and muscular body, she felt like butter left out in the sun, inexorably melting.

All of a sudden he levered himself away from her

and sat back on his haunches. 'What are you doing?' she asked, her mouth going dry at the thought that he had changed his mind and was going to leave.

'I want to look at you,' he replied, and ran his gaze hotly over the feminine curves that she knew were easily revealed by the thin cotton fabric of her nightdress.

She'd put on a little weight since having Matilde, but she knew it suited her...made her more *womanly*, somehow. Dominique scarcely took a breath as Cristiano hooked his thumbs under the flimsy shoestring straps and skimmed them hungrily down over her breasts. Exposure to the air hardened her aching, tingling nipples almost to the point of pain, and she was so turned on by the ravenous glance he gave her that she could swear she was suddenly on fire with a fever. Her thighs trembled and her nipples puckered tighter still, as though he had drawn ice cubes across them. Everything in her was almost unbearably sensitive to every glance, every touch, and she wanted him so much she almost cried.

'Undo your hair for me,' he commanded, his voice sounding as if it rolled over gravel.

With shaking fingers, Dominique slipped off the band from the end of her plait and with long practice deftly released the entwined silken skeins of honeyed brown so that they spilled across her shoulders like a river of tarnished gold. Catching her hair in his hand, Cristiano turned it over again and again to examine it, as though he could not quite believe what he was seeing. Then he raised his glance to meet hers, and in that moment Dominique truly felt as though she was the most beautiful and desired woman on earth—because his dark smouldering gaze told her that she *was*.

Bending his head, he touched his lips to every exposed inch of flesh on her body, then employed his fingers to seductively caress the place where Dominique longed for him the most. Just before he took her to the very cliff-edge of her resistance he peeled off his boxers and used the protection he had brought to sheath himself.

Clinging on to the hard bunched muscles at the tops of his arms as Cristiano inched inside her, Dominique realised her own muscles were almost rigid with tension at the idea of accepting his full, impressive length into her body. She feverishly wondered if her post-baby condition would give him enough of the pleasure she wished for him.

Sensing her anxiety, he went still for a moment as he regarded her. 'Try to relax, *mi ángel*…I realise it has probably been a long time, and that you might be sensitive, but if you relax it will be easier…*sí?*'

Hearing the genuine concern in his voice, Dominique sighed and stroked her hand down over his chest, the tips of her fingers lingering for a moment on one of his hard, flat nipples.

'I'm only afraid I won't be able to—that because of the baby I might not be so—'

Even now, in the most *intimately* vulnerable situation she could find herself in, she still managed to blush. Leaning forward, Cristiano touched her face, his dark gaze brooding and possessive.

'Everything about you is already giving me the most unbelievable satisfaction and pleasure, *mi ángel*... Nothing about your incredible body could possibly disappoint me. Now, let me return the compliment...'

His hard-trained muscles quivering with the effort of not letting his desire overcome him, Cristiano finally thrust inside Dominique to the hilt, and sensed her hot, silky muscles enfold him like the most exquisite tight glove. His heart all but unravelled at how good it felt being with her like this, and his doubts—for now at least—were jettisoned firmly away.

Tussling with his conscience all evening—even *after* his revelation about Martina to Dominique in the library—he had been plagued by many guilt-ridden thoughts. Thoughts that he would be 'betraying' his cousin's memory or letting his family down in some way should he be with Dominique the way he longed to. But most of all Cristiano had worried that by succumbing to the physical attraction that flared so hotly between them Dominique might ultimately believe he was just *using* her. After all... what could he offer her but uncertainty? What had happened to Martina and their baby had scarred him irreversibly, and he was hardly in a position to promise Dominique anything relationship-wise.

However, in the end, *wild horses could not have kept him away from her.* His desire for her was simply beyond all reason.

Dominique moaned low, her incredible blue eyes glazed with uninhibited sensuality as Cristiano drove himself into her again and again with increasing need and passion—certain he could not hold out against this almost unbearable barrage of the senses for much longer without reaching the destination his whole body was primed for. Sensing the sudden rapid constriction of the soft velvet enclave that held him, Cristiano saw Dominique squeeze her eyes shut tight, and passionately he went deeper as she climaxed, causing her to clutch his hips tight and release his name in one of the sexiest-sounding sighs he had ever heard.

Unable to hold back any longer, his will-power and desire finally sent him hurtling upwards into a vortex of pleasure so profound that Cristiano sensed himself unravelling as though he might never stop. The sensation was like the most heart-pounding ride through dizzying white water rapids that he could ever imagine.

'*Madre mia!*'

'Are you all right?'

The ravishing girl in his arms was looking slightly concerned, and Cristiano smiled at her wryly, thinking whimsically that she resembled a beautiful fairy princess from tales of myth and legend with her long rippling hair and bewitching eyes. *She had certainly woven a spell around him...* There could not be many men alive who would resist such shimmering and innocent beauty given the chance, Cristiano speculated.

'All right?' he answered, his glance gently mocking. 'Do you know how you have made me feel? *Estupendo!* Wonderful! Like I could climb a mountain or walk the Great Wall of China non-stop without rest! You have made me a slave to your beautiful sexy body, Dominique, an addict for the taste of your sweet honeyed lips... And most of all...' He sensed the catch in his throat as he coiled some of her dazzling hair round his fingers. 'You have made me hungry for more!'

I think I'm in love. Regarding the gorgeous sable-haired Spaniard who had just made love to her with all the passion and wild beauty that her wounded heart could ever have hoped for, Dominique had the stunning revelation that that same heart was even more vulnerable than she'd feared. Because it was too late now for regrets, or to rein in her emotions where Cristiano was concerned—even if he expected her to. And how was she supposed to stay here in his house, with his family, knowing that her love for him would probably never be reciprocated? That his heart belonged for ever to his wife and baby who had died so tragically?

Anguished, she knew she had probably landed herself in the deepest hot water that she had ever been in—and that *included* becoming an unmarried mother. She'd thought she had found a safe haven at last from all the past hurt that had wounded her, and the thought that she might have to leave that haven practically as soon as she'd arrived made her feel sick to her stomach.

All she could do was leave the outcome to a greater force than her own mere will. Learning to trust again was not something that came easily after what she had been through, but why not give it a try for once? she thought.

As the moonlight beaming in from the open window touched Cristiano's head and shoulders with an almost ethereal glow—and with Christmas just around the corner—she asked herself if there had ever been a better time in which to make a heartfelt request of the Divine?

CHAPTER TEN

THE sensation of a silky hirsute leg rubbing up and down one of her own bare legs beneath the bedclothes caused Dominique's eyes to ping open in heart-racing shock. Caught between the land of sleep and wakefulness, for a moment she forgot where she was.

As the beautiful bedroom with all its fine antiques and luxurious furnishings came into view in the softly smudged morning light—instead of the shabby bedsit she'd grown used to—reality hit with a vengeance. And—more importantly—the reality of just *whose* leg was rubbing up and down against hers.

Turning her head, Dominique came face to face with a pair of smouldering dark eyes that would warm up a statue on a freezing winter's night. And right now, with the look Cristiano was giving her, Dominique was anything *but* an inanimate block of stone…

'*Buenos diás.*' He smiled, placing a deliberately sexy little kiss on her startled mouth.

'I thought—'

'What did you think?' He cupped her face and his leg inserted itself silkily between her thighs.

The melting sensation that made her feel like marshmallow was stealing through her body again, and Dominique struggled to give her thoughts voice. 'I thought—I didn't expect to find you still here,' she admitted, and there was a husky cadence to the words that finally emerged.

'Did you want me to leave?' he asked, tanned brow furrowing.

'No... It's just that...' Struggling to contain her embarrassment, Dominique sighed. 'I thought you might not want anyone else to know... That we were together, I mean.'

'Why would you think that? Do you imagine I am ashamed of being with you?'

'No... But—what will your family think when they find out, Cristiano? What if they think that I deliberately—?'

'Seduced me?' he interjected, his dark brows wriggling comically like a pantomime villain.

Despite her anxiety, Dominique couldn't help but smile. 'I just want them to know that I'm not some manipulative little gold-digger. I would die if I thought they believed that for even a second!'

'If you *were* a gold-digger, do you think you would even be here right now? Do you not think I would have recognised that right from the start? You did not even want to *talk* to me when I first came to your flat! Much less try and get money from me!'

'As long as your family know I am only here because of Matilde…because I don't want her to miss out on having a family who really love her.'

'I do not even have to tell them that… They can already see for themselves the kind of woman you are, Dominique.'

'And they do know that I didn't deliberately get pregnant to try and trap Ramón? It was an accident, you see. He—'

'I do not want to talk about Ramón!'

The anger in Cristiano's voice as well as the tension that rolled off his body, made Dominique recoil for a moment.

'I am only too aware of how my reckless cousin could behave. You do not have to draw me a picture! I am sorry if it hurts you to hear it, but it is a wonder he did not father many more children out of wedlock than just Matilde! Deep in her heart Consuela knows it too.'

'It doesn't hurt me.' Her slender shoulders lifted and fell in a weary shrug. 'Not any more. Please don't be angry because I brought up the subject. I just want things to be out in the open…for there to be no doubt I'm here for all the right reasons. I was just afraid of what Consuela and the others would think if they found out we had slept together. You must understand my fears?'

Driving his hand through his already tousled black hair, Cristiano looked thoughtful for a moment. 'No one is going to think any less of you, Dominique. You will have to trust me on that. In fact, I know they will be glad that I have such a close bond with you. There is nothing to worry about. Truly. Now, come here... Have I not said that I will protect you and take care of you?'

He dropped another lingering kiss on her softly parted lips, as if to seal his assertion, and a sigh of pleasure helplessly left her. But at the back of Dominique's mind she wondered exactly what Cristiano meant by vowing to protect and take care of her. After making passionate love to her for most of the night, did he still view her welfare as something he was interested in merely out of a sense of duty and honour, because his cousin had made her pregnant and her child was a Cordova?

Even though his arm was lying possessively across her middle, Dominique moved to push up into a sitting position. *If the truth were known, Cristiano was probably just as commitment-shy as his cousin.* Doubly so because of what had happened to his wife... Her stomach turned over in dismay. Her wish that there might be a chance for them to enjoy a proper relationship was probably just a foolish pipedream, and one she should quickly put aside unless she wanted to make herself thoroughly miserable. It was nearly Christmas, and she at least wanted the opportunity to try and enjoy the season in this magical place before she had to face any more heartbreaking reality.

'What are you doing?'

'I need to put the bottle warmer on for Matilde's feed.' She glanced down at the wristwatch she wore out of habit most nights. 'She'll be waking up soon.'

Grasping the swathe of silken hair that spilled down over her breasts, Dominique started to swiftly plait it. At the same time, she glanced over to where her baby lay in peaceful slumber.

Cristiano slid his arm coaxingly round her waist. 'She is not awake yet. There is still time to wish each other good morning properly....*sí*?'

His warm lips found the spot between Dominique's shoulder and neck and his teeth nipped gently. Her treacherous body responded immediately, her breasts growing heavy and her nipples stinging with avaricious need to feel his hands and mouth there. But, as delicious as Cristiano's seductive touch was, she knew she was going to have to distance herself a little today out of sheer self-preservation. *Making love with him had left Dominique much more vulnerable to being hurt by him than before, when their relationship had been purely platonic...* He had rocked her world to its innermost core, and the repercussions were already making themselves felt.

'I'm a little...tender,' she told him. It was no contrived excuse. Her lover had been mindful of her welfare, but at times passion had dictated he was not always as gentle as he might have been.

'I am sorry if I hurt you, *mi ángel*... Forgive me.' Cristiano's glance was rueful. 'Next time I will try not to be so demanding. But I cannot minimise the passionate effect your beautiful body has on me, Dominique... Not when every touch makes me burn for more and robs me of the desire and will to even get out of your bed today!'

Thrilling at hearing him say there would be a *next time*, Dominique stored away the little bubble of joy that burst inside her and scooted to the edge of the bed.

'I'll go and sort out the bottle warmer, then get a quick shower before Tilly wakes.'

'Very well.' Behind her, Cristiano lay back on the pillows with his arms over his head, deliberately— or so it seemed to Dominique's hungry eyes—*not* pulling up the sheet to cover his awesome bare chest, as if to show her what she was missing. 'If you *must* desert me I will lie here until my other favourite girl awakes!'

* * *

Everyone seemed in particularly high spirits that morning, and Cristiano was no exception. Being with Dominique and Matilde—or Tilly, as her mother so affectionately called her—affected him profoundly. Apart from arousing his deepest male instincts to take care of them both, just being in their presence lifted him out of the dour and humourless mood that for too long a time since Martina's death had been an unhappily frequent visitor.

Now, as he instructed the crew that were so carefully carrying the huge Christmas tree into the family living room as to where the tree should be placed, he found himself anticipating Dominique's childlike awe when she saw it with mounting pleasure. And when he was alone again after the men had gone, and his mother, aunt, sister and Dominique were all in the kitchen, helping to prepare food for the family's special 'arrival of the tree' lunch, Cristiano allowed himself a few moments of quiet reflection about what had occurred the previous night.

In Dominique's arms he had not just found the physical satisfaction his body craved, he had also found a woman who—although she had been badly betrayed—had not closed the door on being with a man again, and had given him a tantalising glimpse of what it could be like if Cristiano were to commit to her on a permanent basis. His nights would be filled with the most intensely passionate loving, he didn't doubt. And his days—his days would be filled with thoughts of going home to her loving arms whenever he was away from her, and when he was with her he would not want for anything but her and sweet Matilde.

The idea was temptation personified... Yet even as he considered it Cristiano knew a most terrible dark fear as well—the fear of losing Dominique and Matilde as he had lost Martina and their baby, and also Ramón, another family member he had vowed to watch out for and protect. *What if he failed Dominique and her child as he had failed them?* It did not bear contemplating. Cristiano knew he would be drained of everything if that happened. Every positive, hopeful aspect to his life would be gone. He had already been down one of the darkest roads of life, and he did not want to go down one as soul-destroying again. For the sake of his sanity he could not risk it. He simply could not...

'Your mother told me I could come and take a peek.'

The woman Cristiano had been contemplating with such passionate fervour arrived in the room with her baby in her arms, and the vivid blue eyes that could rarely conceal her feelings were already alight with wonder at the sight of the magnificent Christmas tree.

'Oh, Cristiano! It's so beautiful—and the smell

of pine is just divine! But it's so high! How on earth are we going to put the fairy or the star on the top?'

His arm automatically sliding round her slender waist, Cristiano grinned, planted a loud kiss on the baby's downy cheek and then did the same to her wide-eyed mother. 'Some poor idiot will no doubt have to risk a broken neck to climb up a ladder and place it there—that is how!'

'Oh!'

'You may well say oh, *señorita*!'

Unable to resist her adorable expression, Cristiano kissed Dominique again—only this time his mouth moved over her lips instead of her cheek and lingered there. They had the completely ravishing taste of vanilla and honey combined, and he passionately wished that he could take her back to bed and stay there for the rest of the day.

'Cristiano?'

'Hmm?'

'I have a favour to ask…'

'Of course.'

At that moment Cristiano would gladly have given this woman the world if he could. Glimpsing both hope and excitement in her otherwise serious expression, he felt a flare of warmth fill his belly.

'I need to buy some gifts…for your family. Would you be able to take me somewhere so that I could do some Christmas shopping?'

He was about to easily agree when he remembered something.

'Elena is going into town this morning…she mentioned it to me earlier. And we are having a late lunch today, as opposed to an early one, so there is plenty of time. You should go with her. She would be glad to take you, and it would be nice for you to spend some time together on your own. Matilde can stay here with me. Here…let me take her.'

Having no qualms whatsoever about taking care of the infant he was becoming more and more attached to as the days went by, Cristiano put out his arms for the smiling baby. When Dominique released her, Matilde babbled away at him as though certain he understood her perfectly. After positioning her small body safely against his chest, he reached down into his back pocket for his wallet.

'You will need some money,' he said, taking out several notes and holding them out to Dominique.

'No, I won't!' She looked aghast. 'At least, not yours! I do have some money of my own, you know! Do you think I would seriously contemplate buying your family presents with money *you* gave me?'

Knowing she had her principles about things— one of them apparently being to take as *little* as possible from Cristiano—he slowly and reluctantly returned the notes to his wallet and placed it back in his pocket. But, again, he needed to let her know that it was her *right* to be supported and helped by him.

'I did not mean to offend you, *querida*…I merely wanted you to have what you needed without worry. Tomorrow, when I return to my office, I want you to come and meet me for lunch. Elena will bring you. When you are there I will take you over to the bank and set up an account for you to use straight away. I will also get you to sign some legal documents which will give you access to Ramón's money and assets, which—as I explained before— you and Matilde are now entitled to.'

She flushed at that, and Cristiano sensed the mental tussle going on behind those clear blue eyes about accepting something she perhaps believed she did not deserve. He personally knew plenty of people—especially in his line of work—who were definitely *not* possessed of such admirable humility when it came to taking what they believed was due to them. *They could learn a lot from Dominique, he was certain…* Frankly, it still astonished him that she expected so little from her baby's father's family.

'Are you sure you'll be all right with Matilde?' Capturing the end of her plait and staring down at it for a moment, she obviously thought the whole situation was too awkward to comment on further. 'I've left her bottle in the kitchen with Consuela, and there's also a bag with all her baby stuff in. Everything you'll need is there.'

'We will be absolutely fine…won't we, *pequeña?*' Gently he drew the pad of his thumb across the deep little cleft in the infant's chin and grinned with delight when she grabbed his thumb and tried to chew it. 'Just go and enjoy your Christmas shopping, and I will look forward to seeing you at lunch.'

'All right…and thank you.'

'You are most welcome.' His gaze met and held Dominique's with sudden unguarded longing and, seeing by her rapt expression that she felt the same exquisite demand in her body too, he willed her to go find his sister before he dispensed with common sense entirely and persuaded, even *begged* her to come back to bed with him instead…

'It is very sweet of you to want to buy my family gifts for Christmas, but they really do not expect it, you know!' Stirring her coffee, Elena studied Dominique with a concerned frown as she sat across the table from her in the small busy café.

Glancing down at the two shiny carrier bags at her feet, Dominique sighed contentedly. She had taken enormous pleasure in spending the small amount of cash she had kept by for just this purpose, and would not be denied the satisfaction it gave her. The Spanish town was littered with the most individual and interesting little shops, selling everything from ceramics and lace to wood carvings and swords. The art of sword-making had not died out with their Moorish ancestors, Elena had told her. It still thrived today.

Browsing alone for a while, when Elena had left her to do some shopping of her own, Dominique had loved the sense of freedom and excitement it gave her. For once she was anticipating Christmas with something close to joy. Apart from being with Cristiano, she would also be spending it with people who genuinely desired her and her baby's company and cared about their welfare. The small, inexpensive items she'd bought would not bowl anyone over, but it was the thought that counted, and Dominique had wanted some way of saying thank you for the hospitality and total loving acceptance that had been accorded her and Matilde since their arrival.

'It's just my way of thanking all of you for welcoming me and my daughter into your home.'

'You were Ramón's girlfriend and Matilde is his child… You are family whether you wish to be or not!' Elena's dark eyes twinkled. 'And I am also very happy to see that you and my brother are getting along so well too. It has been quite some time since I have seen his eyes light up the way they do when *you* walk into the room, Dominique!'

Feeling her face grow hot beneath the other

woman's teasing and if she was honest surprising observation, Dominique stared.

'It doesn't bother you?'

Elena's smile ebbed away and her expression became more serious. 'Why should it bother me that my brother appears to have found something to make him smile again after so long of being so unhappy it would break your heart?'

'He told me about what happened to his wife and baby.' Lowering her gaze for a moment, Dominique hoped she had not transgressed some unspoken family code by mentioning it. But Elena did not look put out in any way.

'The loss utterly devastated my brother,' she confided. 'And since losing our father he has felt much responsibility for everyone...*too* much. When Martina and the baby died he somehow believed he could have done something to prevent it. I told him, "You are not God! You do not have the power to say whether someone should live or die!" These things happen, and it is terrible for those who are left behind, but perhaps it was Martina's time...you know what I mean? Perhaps it was Ramón's time too. Who knows?'

Shrugging her shoulders in her navy linen dress, Elena sighed, and the deep sadness in her demeanour was palpable. Inside, Dominique's mind and heart were under serious siege at what she had just heard. It was heartbreaking enough that Cristiano had lost his wife and baby in such a shocking way, but to be living with such guilt for what had happened was almost *more* heart-rending.

No wonder he had seemed initially so reluctant to discuss his marriage when Dominique had been studying the photo in the library and had seen him wearing a wedding ring! He had received a great emotional wound and was obviously still in the process of trying to heal. How that healing must be hampered by the idea that he could somehow have prevented his wife's death—and Ramón's death, as Elena had mentioned? How would his poor heart ever heal if he thought their deaths were due to some imagined fault or lapse in his vigilance? What a terrible burden for *anyone* to be carrying round!

'I can't believe what you've just told me, Elena.' Dominique reached out her hand for the other woman's and held it for a few moments in silent solidarity. 'Your brother is a wonderful man, and he doesn't deserve for the rest of his life to be so unhappy because he feels responsible for the people he loved who have died!'

'We have tried telling him that so many times but he does not listen!' Shaking her head a little forlornly, suddenly Elena looked straight at Dominique. 'Perhaps…because it is clear that you and little

Matilde have won a special place in his heart…
perhaps he will listen to *you*, Dominique? Do you
think you could try talking to him about this?'

to...
Matilde...

CHAPTER ELEVEN

*SHE had never seen such a lovingly decorated and
beautiful Christmas tree before.* Dominique was
certain. Standing in front of it that evening with
Matilde, the sparkling lights and glittering baubles
shiningly reflected in her baby daughter's eyes,
Dominique shook her head in silent awe.

The rest of the family had dispersed after a happy
and companionable couple of hours dressing the
tree, and she welcomed these few minutes on her
own to simply just stand and admire it with Matilde.
All those difficult and emotionally sterile
Christmases she'd spent with her mother faded
away in the light of Dominique's feelings now.
Perhaps it was time to forgive and forget? If there
was ever a time to extend forgiveness then this was
probably the season in which to do it. She would
write her mother a letter…or, better still, phone her.
Life was definitely improving, she would tell her,

and perhaps she would be pleased? With some distance between them, maybe some of the tension that was normally prevalent in their relationship would have eased a little?

'You look deep in thought.'

Startled by that compelling deep voice—she hadn't even heard him enter the room—Dominique let her gaze fall into Cristiano's. As was becoming a habit whenever she saw him, her heart seemed to skip a beat.

'I was just enjoying a quiet few moments with Matilde.'

'Then I am disturbing you?'

He started to back away, and before she knew what she intended Dominique had laid her hand on his shirtsleeve to stop him.

'You're not disturbing me at all.'

She'd spent most of the afternoon thinking about what Elena had told her, about him feeling so responsible for his family tragedies, and she'd longed for an opportunity to talk to him alone.

'But you are *definitely* disturbing me.' He moved in closer, smiling ruefully. 'But then…you always do, Dominique.'

'Can we talk?'

'Something is troubling you?'

'Not exactly. I just—'

'Come and see something with me.'

'What?'

'You will see. Come.'

Finding herself led back out into the cavernous hall outside the huge drawing room, Dominique sucked in her breath at the candlelit nativity scene that had been arranged there. Even Matilde stared at it, her little face alive with interest in the small perfectly made figures—both human and animal—amid the straw. Feeling Cristiano's arm slip very naturally round her waist, Dominique knew a stunning moment when everything in her life seemed to suddenly mirror the most exquisite perfection. With her baby in her arms and the man she loved beside her, she was very close to crying with happiness—not to mention relief and joy.

'It's one of the most beautiful things I've ever seen,' she sighed.

'*Sí,*' Cristiano agreed, a faint smile touching his lips. 'This, for me, is what Christmas is all about… this and being with my family.'

'Family is very important to you, isn't it?'

'Of course.'

'Cristiano…Elena mentioned to me today that you've been carrying around so much guilt about what happened to your wife and Ramón. I was sad to hear it. You have no need to feel guilty in any way.'

Her heart was beating so loudly that the roar of it was like an ocean in Dominique's ears. It was too late to take back the statement, but in one sense she wished she could—because, seeing the forbiddingly angry expression that had stolen over Cristiano's face, she knew that the exquisite moment she'd been blessed with just now had suddenly been relegated to bittersweet history. Now she clearly saw the bleak landscape that resided in his compelling eyes, instead of the calm sea that had previously been there, and when his arm left her waist Dominique was utterly bereft.

'So this is what you discussed during your shopping trip?' His mouth tightened in distaste. 'I did not realise it was open season on casual discussion of my feelings!'

Horror-struck, Dominique tightened her arms round her baby's small body, afraid she might drop her because she was trembling so. 'That's not how it was at all! The subject only came up because we care about you, Cristiano! Elena has obviously seen what you've been going through first hand, and she's concerned at how you've been coping.'

'I do not need anybody's concern! What happened was a terrible tragedy and I am coping with it in my own way—a way that does not require anyone else's help or opinions on how I should be dealing with it! I am getting on with my life and I am doing my best to put the event behind me. I would ask that you would respect both my privacy *and* my feelings, Dominique, and not raise the matter again!'

When Cristiano looked as if he might underline his angry statement by walking away from her, Dominique steeled herself with new resolve. She cared about this man far too much to leave him be and let him deal with his tragic loss in isolation, and worse still *blaming* himself for it. After all…he hadn't left *her* alone when she'd insisted she didn't need his help, had he? Whether he knew it or not Cristiano needed her love and support, and she would get that point across if it killed her!

'Are you going to blame yourself for your wife and Ramón's death for the rest of your life, Cristiano?' she burst out.

'Who knows?' He shrugged, his expression bleak as a Siberian winter. 'Maybe I *deserve* to feel guilt? Did you ever ask yourself that…huh? My wife clearly felt she could not confide in me and so the fault *is* mine! Somehow I must have put out the message that she could not have trusted me with the knowledge of the risk she was taking by becoming pregnant…that I would have used the information against her!'

'And would you have?'

'*Sí!* I would! If it meant that she would have had her life, of course! But I am not a tyrant! I knew how much she wanted a baby. If she had told me the truth we could have explored other avenues…like adoption. I wanted children too, but I would not have had her put her life at risk to bear my child!'

'Of course you wouldn't! I know enough about you to realise that, and your family does too!' Her throat aching at the pain he must be feeling, Dominique found it almost too hard to speak. 'Your wife was an adult and she made her own decisions. You have to somehow make your peace with that and absolve yourself of all blame and guilt. I am certain she would have wanted that for you!'

'And what about Ramón?' Moving restlessly away from her, Cristiano walked down the corridor and back again.

'*What* about Ramón?'

'He needed help. He needed *my* help! But I was always too quick to judge him. I always expected the worst, and so what could he do but live up to my limited expectations? He was not a bad person. He was just a boy who missed his father and grew up amongst women who doted on him because they loved him and perhaps spoiled him a little too much. I could see that it grieved him that he could not please me the way he wanted to. He was so hungry to be what the world thought of as a success, and he was not happy that instead he was viewed as a spoiled rich boy who had neither sense nor morals! I have thought many times about his accident…I have wondered if in a state of depression he might have deliberately driven his car too fast that night along that treacherous road… That he might have—'

'Taken his own life?' Her eyes widening, Dominique vehemently shook her head. 'Ramón would never have done such a thing! No matter what might have been going on with him, he loved life far too much to want to end it! Cristiano, you must have been driving yourself crazy with all these wild imaginings! You've got to let this go…please! For your *own* sake if not for your family's! Because it would be a terrible shame—and not only that such a tragic waste too—if you were to continue to burden yourself with all this useless guilt!

'Who knows how much time any of us are given when we arrive in this world? Crippling ourselves with "if onlys" is futile when we don't ultimately control *any* of it! I am sure you were an amazing husband to Martina, and the best of cousins to Ramón—but you had nothing to do with the reasons they died! And if they loved you—as I am certain they must have—do you think they would want the rest of your life to be blighted with unhappiness because you believe you could have done something to prevent their passing?'

'It is not so easy to just let go of the guilt, as you suggest.' His dark eyes glittering, Cristiano's sculpted features were taut with pain. 'When my father died it fell to me to take on the mantle of head of the family. That entails being someone they can rely and depend on! They told me at the hospital afterwards that Martina had always carried a high risk of having complications in childbirth—she had pleaded with the doctors not to tell me about it! Can you imagine? She carried that burden all by herself, when if she had shared it with me I could have—'

'Saved her?' Dominique didn't know how she dared even say the words when the man in front of her seemed so furious, but say them she had to. 'Think about what you're saying, Cristiano… please! You are a wonderful man, dependable and reliable—the kind of man anyone would want on their side—but that doesn't mean you have the power to control every single event that happens in your loved ones lives or your own! I'm sure your wife only wanted to spare you pain by not telling you about her condition. She must have loved you *so* much. Ramón too. He had a car accident, Cristiano. Accidents happen every day. How could you possibly have had anything to do with that? It was in his nature to take foolish risks sometimes, with no regard for his safety! I knew him too, remember? But you, Cristiano…you have the whole of the rest of your life ahead of you, and you have to forgive yourself for the imagined failings in your past and move on… Just as *I* am learning to move on.'

Silence fell. A silence broken only by the harsh drawn-out breaths that came from Cristiano. Praying she hadn't somehow made things worse by speaking out, Dominique could only wait in sound-less anguish for the outcome of their passionate exchange. In her arms Matilde wriggled, and then let out a sharp cry. Her attention diverted, Dominique tenderly touched her lips to her baby's velvet-soft forehead.

'What is it, my darling? Are you hungry? Is that what's wrong?'

'Go and feed the child.'

The tiniest flicker of a smile raised the corners of Cristiano's mouth. He looked resigned and a little weary, perhaps, but not angry any more. A shaft of the most dizzying hope raced through Dominique's insides.

'Will you come with me?' she asked.

He sighed heavily. 'Not right now. I need some time alone to think. But we will talk again later, I promise.'

Wishing fiercely that he would change his mind and join her, Dominique tried to corral her frustra-tion and give him a smile. 'Well…when your thinking is done, perhaps you'll come and find me?'

Giving her an enigmatic smile in return, Cristiano turned his back and walked away down the corridor…

* * *

He drove for miles, hardly paying attention to where he was going. Somehow the act of driving, of steering the car and working the controls, helped free his mind so that he could think with more clarity. It was said that Einstein had had his best and most creative thoughts when he was shaving. Cristiano allowed himself a small grin at this, one of the more obscure facts he'd collected over the years. Then, as a bundle of dried grasses rolled by in the warm gusty wind, his expression grew more serious again.

The emotionally charged encounter he'd had with Dominique while admiring the belén *had struck a loud chord inside him.* For a man who had once given absolute credence to the idea that there was a purpose and a meaning to every life it was amazing how he could have gone so wildly off course with his guilt-ridden beliefs. Dominique, his mother, Consuela and Elena—they had *all* been right in their assertion that the power to control events did *not* lie with him…as it did not lie with *any* man or woman, for that matter. That being the case, there *was* no blame.

He had always done his best for the people he loved. *Always.* If it still nagged at him a little that perhaps he should have made himself more available to talk to Ramón than he had done then

Cristiano told himself it was about time he let that thought go and realised that even if he *had* spent more time with his troubled cousin he probably would not have been able to change anything. Just as knowing what Martina had faced would not have changed anything either. His wife had always longed for children. Even if Cristiano had persuaded her that with the risks involved it was probably not a good idea for her to become pregnant she would have fought him tooth and nail to get her own way. And if he had tried to stop her she would have been dreadfully unhappy, possibly even blamed him for not letting her try to have a baby.

In the end, it was just not meant to be... Letting out a deep sigh to free the sensation of tightness in his chest, Cristiano focused on the dusty road ahead, the glorious sight of the sun-struck mountains giving a little ease to the painful emotions that beset him. Dominique was right. *She had learned some hard lessons in her own life and had not emerged from them without gaining some valuable insight.* Nobody knew how much time they were allotted on earth. All one could do was live each day in the best way that they could and trust that there was indeed a plan for everyone.

To Cristiano's mind it now seemed somewhat ungrateful to waste another day of the life he had been given in guilt and regret. Especially when his future could possibly be *far* brighter than he had ever dared to hope…

A wave of tiredness hit her later on that afternoon, and Dominique went to have a lie-down in her bedroom. At Consuela and Luisa's insistence she left the baby with them while she rested.

All she could think about was Cristiano and whether, after what they had discussed, there would be room in his life for her and Matilde after all. Not just as their 'guardian and protector', but as something deeper and more meaningful…something that would require him to make a more lasting commitment to them than he might have envisaged?

If such a thing could not be achieved, then Dominique would have no alternative but to return to England after Christmas and just pay a visit now and again, as she had suggested once before. It was too bad if he did not like that plan. She needed to survive too, and she could not do that if she was around Cristiano without the deep connection between them that she craved…

Worn out with thinking and hoping, she eventually dozed off.

When she came downstairs about an hour later, she found the women gathered together in the drawing room, talking companionably. There was no sign of Cristiano. Elena had told her earlier that he'd gone out for a drive, and Dominique's stomach had been tied up in knots at the idea that he was driving to try and get away from the deep unhappiness that consumed him. *What if he never resolved the guilt and regret that dogged him about his wife's death? What if he remained a widower for the rest of his life, never allowing himself the chance of being with someone new? Someone who adored him with every fibre of her being? Someone who wanted the opportunity to show him how good life could be again?*

Dominique tried for a smile as Consuela dandled Matilde on her knee and made the baby laugh, but she knew it was a half-hearted effort at best.

'You have a nice lie-down?' the older woman asked in her halting English.

'Lovely…thank you. I feel revived.'

Her gaze fell upon the small overnight case that was at Consuela's feet. Recognising it as her own, Dominique frowned.

Observing her quizzical glance, Consuela lifted it by its leather handle and held it out to her. 'You go with Cristiano,' she said, smiling.

'Cristiano?'

'I have been waiting for you, *querida*,' a familiar voice said from behind her.

Standing in the doorway, with a bone-melting smile, dressed in dark trousers, white shirt and a stylish chocolate-brown suede jacket, he was the most devastatingly handsome man on earth, and Dominique's heart all but leapt into her throat at the sight of him.

'I don't understand…'

'I am taking you to Madrid for a little trip. I own a small hotel there. We will stay the night and drive back tomorrow.'

'I sneaked into your room and packed your bag while you slept. I hope you do not mind?' Rising to her feet from her armchair, Elena went to Dominique and gave her a brief but affectionate hug.

'But—but what about Matilde?'

'Need you ask?'

Cristiano grinned, and Dominique looked round at the three women, whose love for her child was shining in each pair of twinkling dark eyes…

'This is all a bit sudden, isn't it?' Her legs were shaking as she realised she was the unsuspecting target of a somewhat tender conspiracy.

Cristiano released a heavy sigh and scraped a hand through his gleaming dark hair. 'Are you going to stand there looking bemused for the rest of the day? Or are you going to come with me and find out what this is all about when we get to Madrid?'

Dominique swallowed hard. 'I think I'm going

to go with you,' she replied, her voice a little husky with emotion.

'*Bien!*'

As he held out his hand, Cristiano's dazzling smile was like sunshine after a prolonged period of rain, and he enfolded her small, slim palm protectively in his own…

'A small hotel, you said?' With her head on one side as she surveyed the sumptuously appointed bedroom in their suite, Dominique glanced wryly at her good-looking companion as he dropped his bag and her overnight case on a chair. 'Define "small", Cristiano?'

'Okay.' He shrugged. 'So I am prone to being a little modest. It is hardly my worst fault!'

'Now that you've mentioned it, what *is* your worst fault?'

Walking slowly towards him, Dominique knew the expression on her face was deliberately provocative. The answering gleam in Cristiano's black eyes made her heart race.

He put his arms out as she reached him and caught her in a possessive embrace. 'Perhaps it is that when I fall in love I fall too hard and too fast?' he said, smoothing the pad of his thumb across her cheek.

Dominique thought she glimpsed a momentary flash of pain cross his sculpted features. 'Has it happened often?' she asked softly.

'No…only twice in my life.' He was staring at her as though she were some kind of priceless treasure just unveiled to him. 'And you?' he enquired, his expression suddenly more intense. 'Were you in love with Ramón?'

'It's like I told you when we first met. I thought I was for a time…' She grimaced at the bittersweet memory. 'But really I just—I just needed someone, and for a while he was there for me.'

'So you have never really been in love?'

'Not until now. No.'

Silence was the answer to her nervously voiced statement, and inside her chest Dominique's heart squeezed with love and longing for the man who was holding her so tenderly and yet at the same time with a grip like steel that promised not to let her easily escape…

'Something inside me died when I lost my wife,' Cristiano told her, and for a long moment she held her breath. 'I truly believed I would never find another woman to replace her…let alone lose my heart again. But you have proved me wrong, Dominique…*so* wrong! I find myself as foolish and as hopeful as a schoolboy when you are around, and all I can think of is taking you somewhere we can be alone together so that I can make love to you!'

'I feel the same! Oh, Cristiano, I love you so much!' Thrilling at his words, yet impatient for him to stop talking so that she could feel that heavenly mouth of his against hers, Dominique put her hand up to his gleaming black hair and gently smoothed a lock of it away from his temple. 'You have become the most important thing to me and Matilde. I don't even want to *imagine* living the rest of our lives without you!'

'Then do not!' Cristiano growled passionately against her ear.

Sensing his hands move down to her hips and drag her hard against his pelvis, Dominique felt the steely hardness of his desire brush urgently against her and her limbs flooded with glorious liquid velvet. 'Take me to bed…*please,*' she whispered back to him.

They undressed urgently, but Cristiano's movements deliberately slowed as he undid Dominique's coiled hair as though unwrapping the most precious of gifts. This was not a task to hurry or take lightly. It was one of the erotic privileges he had so often dreamed of since Dominique had come into his life.

A wave of fierce masculine pride assailed him as he sensed her quiver hard with excitement at his touch. *He was quivering too.* All his senses were wild with joy, and with the hot, restless need to unite his body with hers once again.

The only covering Dominique had when he was finished was her glorious mane of rippling spun gold hair, its dark honey brushing temptingly against the aroused tips of her beautiful breasts as it cascaded down to her slender but nicely rounded hips. Unable to resist touching her a moment longer, Cristiano put his mouth to those delectable rigid points and sucked hard. The sensation caused even more heat to flood straight to his loins, and his erection was so tight with arousal that the line between pleasure and pain was only separated by the slimmest of threads.

Sliding his hand through her hair, he pushed Dominique's head gently down to the plumped-up pillows behind her. When she was lying supine, he moved back down her body, parted her long smooth thighs and slid his fingers across the hot, silky nub at her centre. She immediately jerked, and panted out his name. Caught up in the fast-flowing river of his growing desire, Cristiano delved deep inside her with hungry fingers, and then, when he was drenched in her honeyed heat, he put his mouth to the place where his fingers had caressed her.

Her thighs moved helplessly wider apart, and Dominique's hands gripped the satin eiderdown beneath her with a groan as Cristiano's tongue moved rhythmically back and forth across the core of her femininity. Just when she thought she would break like an overstretched harp-string if she didn't have the release she ached for Cristiano used that wicked instrument of seductive torment upon her with deliberate erotic slowness, and drenching waves of glorious heat swept over her in tingling succession, endowing her body with the most profoundly wondrous delight it had ever known…

When he glanced up at her with the most toe-curling satisfied grin Dominique had ever seen, desire consumed her again almost in an instant. Fastening her hands on the iron-hard slopes of his broad muscular shoulders, she urged him urgently towards her.

'Now you,' she breathed. 'I want you to have the same pleasure you have just given to me!'

'*Mi amor*… You will not find me arguing with that!'

He slid into her body in one smooth but sure thrust, and Dominique felt her muscles grip him tightly and quiver hard with delight. Her hunger and arousal reached barely imagined peaks of joy as Cristiano drove into her like a man intent on making her remember this amazing connection always. She ran her hands over his back and felt her nails dig into his slick, taut muscles as the feelings inside her grew close to the point of explosion.

When they had both cried out at the same time, their gazes meeting in shared wonder, they slowly returned to earth together, holding on to each other fast.

'I want you to be my wife.'

Without preamble, Cristiano spoke his thoughts aloud.

'Was it your intention to ask me that when you brought me here?' Dominique inquired, her pulse accelerating with the wildest joy.

'Yes, it was.'

'And does your family know you were going to ask me this?'

He shook his head and smiled. 'No. I would not tell them what was in my mind until I spoke to you, *mi ángel*.'

'Are you sure, Cristiano? You'd be taking on a lot, you know. Me *and* Matilde.'

'I love your daughter as if she were my own...I want to be her father, Dominique, but that does not mean I will not tell her anything she wants to know about Ramón when she gets older. Of course I also want *us* to have children together too...maybe three or four...'

'Three or four?' Dominique gasped.

'At *least*!'

'You plan to keep me busy, then?'

'Very!'

With a wicked smile, Cristiano claimed her lips for long, satisfying seconds, and for a while Dominique simply let herself bask in the luxury and delight of his amazing kisses. Then he lifted his head, glancing down at her with a frown.

'You have not said whether you will accept my offer of marriage yet. I beg you not to keep me waiting any longer!'

'Didn't I just give you my answer with my eyes, Cristiano?' Her voice soft with emotion, Dominique slid her palm across his slightly roughened cheek and caressed it. 'Of *course* I will be your wife! I want the chance to show you that life can be good again…for us both. We won't forget the past, but for now we will put it behind us. Our memories will be like a library we visit from time to time, but they will not be where we *live*!'

'*Sí*…I like that.'

And to show her how much he concurred with her statement, Cristiano once again showered his wife-to-be with the kind of kisses that meant they would be most fervently occupied for a considerably long time indeed…

Christmas Eve…

Standing outside Cristiano's study door, Dominique glanced down at her green satin dress with a little spurt of pleasure. Her fiancé had bought it for her only yesterday, insisting that she had to have something special to wear on one of the most celebrated of nights in the Spanish calendar.

In the kitchen, the housekeeper and the rest of the

Cordova women were busily engaged in putting the finishing touches to the splendid feast that was in store—a menu that had been planned with a precision and attention to detail that wouldn't have shamed an army campaign. The house looked absolutely stunning, and it was as if everything around Dominique were holding its breath in anticipation of what was to come. It was indeed turning out to be the kind of Christmas that Dominique had longed for, and one she would remember for ever…

Knocking lightly on the heavy oak door, she felt butterflies immediately assail her insides at Cristiano's almost curt, *'Adelante!'*

'It's only me,' she announced shyly as she stepped over the threshold into the impressive high-ceilinged room.

Seated behind a huge desk, Cristiano glanced up and gave the smile that never failed to turn her legs to jelly. His hungry gaze made no bones about the fact that he very much liked what he saw, and he pushed to his feet and moved across the room to join her.

'Hola…"it's only me"!' he teased. 'I like what you are wearing, by the way. Whoever bought it has impeccable taste!'

'I wanted to give you your Christmas present.' Her closed palm opened to reveal the small package it had been concealing, and Dominique gave the small silver-wrapped box to Cristiano.

She twisted her hands together a little nervously as she watched him peel off the glittery paper and then open the lid of the cardboard container that was inside. As he withdrew the perfectly oval silver frame, he studied the photograph it contained with an almost grave expression on his face. Then he looked up, and Dominique saw that his eyes had a sheen that hadn't been there before.

'Do you like it?' she asked anxiously. 'I couldn't think what else to give you.'

'I love it, *mi ángel!* You could not have given me anything more precious. I will put it on my desk at work, and whenever I need some inspiration I will look at this picture of my two beautiful girls and know that I can accomplish anything if they are by my side…*anything!*'

'I'm so glad you feel that way.'

'Never doubt what I say…I mean *every* word. And now I have something to give to you.'

Walking back to his desk, Cristiano put down the photograph with its wrapping and opened a drawer. Removing something, he walked slowly back to where Dominique stood. Opening what she now saw was a tiny black velvet heart-shaped box, he took out the most dazzling ruby and sapphire ring and, taking Dominique's left hand in his, he placed the glittering jewel on her wedding finger.

'Now you are officially my fiancée!' He beamed

and, pulling her close, kissed her with lingering thoroughness. When he had freed her lips once more, he cupped her face in his hands. 'And soon that ring will be joined by another one…a *wedding* band. Happy Christmas, Dominique. Know that I love you more than I can say. You and Matilde have given my life a meaning I thought never to have again.'

'When we first met, your words drew the most captivating picture of what Christmas was like in your country, and I so longed to experience some of the magic you conveyed! But nothing could have prepared me for the miracle of *you*, Cristiano… *nothing!* Happy Christmas, my love!'

Celebrate 100 years of pure reading pleasure with Mills & Boon®

To mark our centenary, each month we're publishing a special 100th Birthday Edition. These celebratory editions are packed with extra features and include a FREE bonus story.

Plus, you have the chance to enter a fabulous monthly prize draw. See 100th Birthday Edition books for details.

Now that's worth celebrating!

September 2008

Crazy about her Spanish Boss by Rebecca Winters
Includes FREE bonus story
Rafael's Convenient Proposal

November 2008

**The Rancher's Christmas Baby
by Cathy Gillen Thacker**
Includes FREE bonus story *Baby's First Christmas*

December 2008

One Magical Christmas by Carol Marinelli
Includes FREE bonus story *Emergency at Bayside*

Look for Mills & Boon® 100th Birthday Editions at your favourite bookseller or visit
www.millsandboon.co.uk

FREE!
4 Books
and a surprise gift!

We would like to take this opportunity to thank you for reading this Mills & Boon® book by offering you the chance to take FOUR more specially selected titles from the Modern™ series absolutely FREE! We're also making this offer to introduce you to the benefits of the Mills & Boon® Book Club™—

- ★ **FREE home delivery**
- ★ **FREE gifts and competitions**
- ★ **FREE monthly Newsletter**
- ★ **Exclusive Mills & Boon Book Club offers**
- ★ **Books available before they're in the shops**

Accepting these FREE books and gift places you under no obligation to buy, you may cancel at any time, even after receiving your free shipment. Simply complete your details below and return the entire page to the address below. You don't even need a stamp!

YES! Please send me 4 free Modern books and a surprise gift. I understand that unless you hear from me, I will receive 6 superb new titles every month for just £2.99 each, postage and packing free. I am under no obligation to purchase any books and may cancel my subscription at any time. The free books and gift will be mine to keep in any case.

P8ZEF

Ms/Mrs/Miss/Mr ....Initials ....

Surname ....

Address .... **BLOCK CAPITALS PLEASE**

....

....Postcode ....

Send this whole page to:
UK: FREEPOST CN81, Croydon, CR9 3WZ